# Passion From
## Within

~ Riley Brett ~

# Passion From Within

~ *Based on a true story* ~

Copyright © 2020 by Riley Brett

All rights reserved. This book or any portion thereof may not be reproduced or used in any manner whatsoever without the express written permission of the publisher except for the use of brief quotations in a book review.

This book is a work of fiction based on real-life events. All characters and places are a product of the author's imagination basing off of a true story. Any resemblance to actual persons, living or dead is entirely coincidental due to the true story remaining anonymous.

Self-published.

Book cover photo purchased from Stocksy by Amanda Worrall.
Cover design and book editing by Riley Brett.
Cover design inspired by Carl Gawboy.

Book 1

Library of Congress Control Number: 2020920563
ISBN: 978-1-7359146-0-2

*For my grandfather, who gave his anything
to be our everything.*

## Section 1

# 4-years and a step ahead

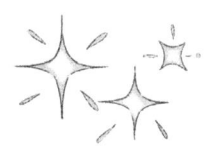

## Chapter 1
# Homeful Wishes

Between the baby blue trim and the worn-down fence, the house doesn't look all that bad. The home needs some remodeling but apart from that, the comforting look gives it a perfect story to be told. Only I wish that were the case. The screaming and bruising from within gives another side to the story…

Screams come traveling down the hallway. Molly pulls her cat in closer, close enough to smell the last kitty treat she had given her. She is doing what she can to not focus on what is going on in her mother's room. She fights her mind to get rid of the screams and cries, yet no matter what she does, they will be forever imprinted in her head.

The vibration of a body being slammed travels through her closet wall, Molly feels it travel throughout her and give a sensation of weakness to the knees. As she sits on her bedroom closet floor she feels water gliding down her rosy cheeks, her eyesight now blurring. She tries to fight the tears but they tremble down her cheeks anyway.

"She'll be ok," Molly whispers to herself, "just like always she will be alive and upbeat in the morning".

Molly figures the more she says it to herself maybe she will start to believe it, but that is never the case. She looks across her room and sees her Tinkerbell table, and wonders if she will ever draw there with her mom again. She decides to push that thought aside, but other horrifying thoughts come flooding in. Another slam hits the wall, her body flinches in fear. Suddenly more tears start to pour down her cheeks, she is now sobbing and praying to god her mom will be ok.

. . .

Molly opens her bright hazel eyes to sunshine flooding into her closet, making her puffed-up face hurt even more. Her cat had fallen asleep on her lap, but she doesn't mind one bit. Molly had gotten the cat for her 3rd birthday and has adored it ever since she tried to name the cat triangle but her mom knew she could think of something better. So Molly with the help of her grandmother named the cat Salvus, the ring of it gave her a safe and comforting feeling.

"Morning Salvus", she whispers.

With a forced smile, she lifts herself along with the cat. She walks over to the bed and sets the cat down. She wants to check on her mom, though she isn't too eager to see what new bruises

~ *Passion From Within* ~

were brought upon her fair skin. Despite all the fears traveling through her head and her limbs, she moves to her door, and she slowly opens it.

There are rays of sunshine shining down the narrow hallway, yet it still feels dark and frightening. Molly inches closer to her mother's bedroom door, her legs are starting to shake and she is beginning to regret the idea. But she carries on, her hand reaches the doorknob and it twists. Peaking her head in, she only sees her mom. Laying there . . . unlively. Her body looks weak and fragile, her fair white skin being magnified by the sunlight peeking through the curtains. Along with the amplification of purple within her bruising.

Molly steps near the bed and spots more bruising on her mother's back, being almost fully covered by her T-shirt. She fights the tears as best as she can. Her throat is getting tight, anger and sadness fill her face and her fists. But she is completely helpless. There is nothing she can do about what happened last night and still nothing she can do to prevent it from happening again. She is only 4. Turning 5 next week won't make the slightest difference.

Molly's tummy is now rumbling. She starts to shake her mom in hopes that she will wake and make breakfast.

"Mom," Molly whispers. "Mom . . . please wake up," she says again, now in a more frightened tone.

Her mom groans and weakly pushes Molly's hand to the side. She is so skinny. The question of why wanders through her mind.

Molly hopes he won't walk in, despite being very brave, he weakens her. Every part of her body folds, even just by the sound of his voice. But she can't leave her mom vulnerable and unattended, she is much more scared of that.

*His* name is Nocens, Noc for short. She can't say it without trembling of fear and anger.

Her gut jolts, instant shivers consume her body. She knows that feeling and is all too familiar with it. Molly quickly turns and sees him standing in the doorway. Her heart stops . . . her face now flooding with warmth, sweat forming in the fold of her palm.

"What are you doing in here?" Noc says in a deep raspy voice.

"I . . . I dunno." Molly manages to reply.

She is now shaking. Emotions are flooding throughout her entire body. She still doesn't want to leave her mom.

*Is she ok?* Molly wonders. *I should ask, I just don't want to upset him.*

"Moll you should be in your room, you're not allowed in here remember?" Noc says, with all of the wrong intentions.

Molly hates that nickname, it makes her feel even more powerless.

"I . . . I'm sorry," she weakly forces out of herself.

*I still can't leave her*, she thinks again. *But I have no choice.*

Molly manages to scramble out of the room, just sliding inches away from his arm. Thumps from her heartbeat pound against her chest, she sprints down the hallway and into her room.

*~ Passion From Within ~*

Her tummy rumbles again as she quickly closes the door. *I could go for some of Papa's homemade pancakes.* She thinks, remembering his magnificent breakfasts. *I miss them . . .*

Molly is very close to her grandparents, she aspires to be like them someday. They both possess wonderful qualities, and they both have characteristics you should carry with you throughout your life. They make a huge impact on her, even at such a young age. Their presence gives her a warm and comforting feeling, they make her simply feel at home.

She sits on her bed next to Salvus, the cat climbs into her lap. Footsteps creak on the floorboards down the hallway. She tenses up, hoping it is her mom and not him. Something peaks out the corner of her eye . . . she sees a white shirt flash by. She can't get a full view due to her door being cracked at an inch.

A raspy voice echoes into her room, but she can't tell whose voice it is and what they're trying to say. She hopes that it is her mother.

*Please god, please.* Molly prays.

The door cracks open . . .

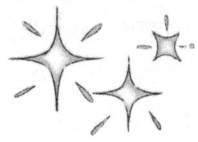

Chapter 2

# Silent Cries

"Molly?" an unsteady voice echoes into Molly's room.

"Mom?" Molly asks.

*Please be mom.* She prays again.

She hops off her bed and starts walking slowly to the door . . .

"Good morning sweetie, how'd you sleep?" her mom says while walking into the room.

Molly jumps. Relief fills her body as she looks into her mother's eyes, they send her a warmth that glides throughout her body letting her know that everything will be ok.

Her mom's name is Genus, but everyone calls her Jen. She is tall and has long thick brown hair with a tint of red. Her eyes green and vibrant, looking into them always makes Molly curious as to what her mother hides within herself from the rest of the world.

~ *Passion From Within* ~

"Uhm . . . good," Molly says.

She forces a smile to confirm the statement. She knows it was a lie, but she doesn't want her mom to know she heard the screams and cries from last night. Molly doesn't want her mom to know that they are now burned in her head, and the trembles will forever leave a chill on her skin.

"Good." her mother replies.

Molly sighs in discomfort. It is hard for her to feel comfortable in a house that consumes such violence and hardship. She refuses to call it her *home*, a home is much different than a house. In her perspective, a home is a place where you feel safe and you always know you can come back to it. This place, this house is far from a home. It doesn't feel safe and when she leaves she dreads returning. When she visits her grandparents she never wants to leave. Just their presence makes her feel at home, and their house has always been a safe place for her to go, no matter what.

Molly's mom leaves the room. She hears another voice, this time it's deeper and it gives her chills. Molly hears mumbled voices run down the hallway, she tries to make out what they are saying.

"I told you not to do that . . ." Noc says aggressively.

Molly can't hear everything they are saying but she can hear parts, just enough to get frightened.

"I . . . I didn't think it mattered." her mother stutters.

"Stop playing dumb and grow up," Noc says in a threatening tone.

". . . sorry, I'll do better next time," she says under her breath.

"What'd you just say to me?" Noc's voice intensely rises. "Are you testing my authority? Because if you are . . ."

"I . . . no of course not . . ." her mother whispers.

A few seconds go by, for Molly they feel like everlasting minutes. A thump hits the ground and vibrates under her little feet. Her skin covers with goosebumps and spiked up hairs. She falls to the floor, her limbs have given her no choice. Her emotions are slowly taking over in a protective manner. Since this feeling is ever so familiar, her body knows the drill and the precautions to take. Yet not all the precautions can protect her from the inevitable mental scaring.

She runs to pick up Salvus and bolts off to her bed. She lays there trembling with fear and in desperate need of help. She doesn't know if she has enough courage to run into her mother's room and save her from the torturous beating. It is hard to imagine the amount of pain she would be in if it was her own father beating on her mother.

Jen's scream echoes down the narrow hallway, Molly can hear the pain within her mother's voice. She cannot get the pain-filled scream out of her head, it is replaying itself over and over. She does everything she can to try and get rid of the scaring scream but nothing is working, it has embedded itself within Molly. Thudding continues on the floorboards and it vibrates throughout her bed.

"... I told you this would happen again. Don't go making this a daily routine now Jen." Noc yells aggressively as he beats upon her mother's body.

Her mom attempts to run down the hallway, away from the hell filling room of hers. But Noc catches up and drags her back into the room, their door slams shut causing the walls to shake.

Mumbled voices continue. Molly and her mother are in desperate need of any kind of help, anything at all.

Tears begin to flood down her uncomfortable flaring cheeks. So many tears flood down her cheeks on the daily it is basically her day to day routine.

*Day after day I have no voice nor control.* She admits to herself. *I need to do something I can't just sit here while my mom is going through this. But what am I going to do? I am scared, not only for mom but for me too.*

Molly hears more thumping and clashing, but slowly it starts to fade away...

Slowly all that is left is the intense vibration rattling through the walls and floors. Molly is starting to experience her mind going numb. All her emotions combining into a single feeling of emptiness. No single emotion, just a feeling. Molly doesn't know what is happening to her and why she cannot form words in her own mind. Everything is blank. She cannot speak, she cannot think, she cannot move, she is entirely numb. The pain is paralyzing her body, one traumatic experience at a time.

How could a 4-year-old know how to persevere through this? Salvus slowly walks next to Molly, she grabs ahold of the cat and starts to feel slightly less alone. She feels, she feels the presence of Salvus and how it brings her comfort and safety. Molly is slowly starting to gain emotion, even if it is a small amount she will take all that she can get. Salvus gives her that power, the power to believe in herself, to believe in her own strength and capabilities. The cat is her reassurance of what strength she truly possesses even if she doesn't always feel it, it's there. Crazy how a cat can obtain such a powerful role in a little girl's life.

Clashing objects and mumbled voices continue down the hall. The vibration throughout the wall and floorboards carry on. Molly attempts to distract herself by playing with stuffies . . . though her mind ignores the weak attempt of distraction and continues to dwell on the worries.

*What if this is the last time?* She thinks. *What if something happens to her, what will I do, where will I go? What if he decides to come. . .to come hurt me?*

She stops herself from finishing the thought. There are far too many what if's that are all too realistic, it makes her sick to her stomach. There must be someone who can help, somebody who can protect us. Unless this is normal and Molly is just overreacting. It is hard to believe that this is a normal feeling to have but how would she know this either? This is all she has ever grown to know.

A door knob screeches down the hall. Her heart drops in fear and worry.

~ *Passion From Within* ~

*If I stay quiet maybe he won't remember that I am here*, she thinks. *Please don't come in here* . . .

Footsteps approach her room, then quickly pass. The stairs begin to creek, with each step furthering away. Quiet sobs continue in Jen's room, a pain-filled cry weeps out. The pain is consuming her mother's body in ways she can not understand.

*Mom. What's wrong with her, did he hit her too hard?* She wonders deeply.

Molly debates running into her mother's room to check on her. Tires screech outside the house, she walks over to her window and watches Noc drive off.

*He's gone.* She watches the car drive off. *Please don't come back* . . .

She remembers her mom and quickly runs down the hallway with heavy pressure on her chest.

"Mom? Mom are . . . you ok?" she asks softly. Looking along her mother's skin she sees all kinds of bruising. Between her mother's thin body and the bruising upon her ever so fair skin, she looks as if she was a fragile object ready to crack at any second to come.

"Mom . . . please don't cry. It will be ok . . ." sobs tighten Molly's throat, making it hard to speak, even harder to breathe.

Although Molly doesn't know that for sure, she doesn't want her mom to be in such pain. She grabs onto her mom almost feeling every bone beneath her skin. Squeezing not too tight in fear she might hurt her mother's weak hands. Watching as her mother tries to hold back the sobs.

"I'm ok . . . sweety. We were . . . we were jus . . . just wrestling." her mother says shakily.

Molly gathers all of her strength and holds back the tears as best she can because her mom said it was just wrestling. *It's fine, she's fine, I just overreacted.* She tries to convince herself, partly trying to make herself believe it to be true. *Why is she crying so hard? I don't cry that hard when I lose a game.*

"Why are . . . why are you so sad?" Molly asks, staring curiously into her mother's eyes.

"Well . . . I lost." her Mom answers weakly.

"Why did you cry so hard? Was it an important game?"

"Uhm . . . yea . . . yeah, it was an important one."

Molly looks deeper into her mother's eyes, still hand in hand. She squeezes her mother's hand and feels bones collide. Jen's eyes are red and watery, full of pain and cluelessness. A tear slips down Molly's cheek and slides into the crevice of her dimpled chin. She turns her face away from her mother, trying to hide the tears, she lets go of her mother's hand and steps away. She begins to speed walk into her room, where she rests with silent cries weeping from her body. Funny how pain can take so many different forms. The cries from Molly is mental pain beginning its scaring structure in her little 4-year-old innocent body. And of course, she has no idea what is slowly happening to her.

. . .

Hours pass by, to Molly, it feels like days. The last few hours were spent playing with toys which inclued Salvus cutting in and being the destructor of "Strawberry short cake's Town", her favorite game. Along with drawing pictures alone at her Tinkerbell table, wondering if her mom is ok. No matter how hard she tries to distract herself from the pain, she feels it anyway. She can't help but worry about her mom, no matter how many toys she gathers, none will do the job to distract her mind. Although she worries, she continues to play with her toys and doesn't fully engage with the fear.

Molly walks down the stairs, with every step a stair creaking. She continues towards the kitchen in the hope to find some kind of food that she can prepare for herself. Not every day is like this, there was a time when everything was more livable than it was bearable. . .

Her father Sam and her brother little Sam Jr. used to live with Molly and Jen. Molly spent every waking moment following her brother, fascinated by everything he did. They played with little toy cars, watched spider-man, rode scooters until the sky was almost fully dark, ate pancakes, got in trouble for arguing (rarely), and played around late-night fires in the backyard. He gave her someone to run around aimlessly with, simply the chance to *be a kid*. Her father gave her the unconditional love that she was only beginning to learn about, and the simple but extravagant adventures she craved severely which included going to carnivals and car shows. At one point in time, he even dressed as a clown, Molly made fun of him for weeks because of how red his nose was and how it made him look extremely silly. All of that, every single moment with life filling potential wiped away as Nocens entered their life. Pushing her father to the side and bringing in his own idea of a future, leaving Molly with heartache and confusion. From what she remembers it was everything she could have wanted, and wish to still have.

All of those moments leading to now, opening the fridge and finding processed cheese squares and raw hot dogs instead of leftover Mac & Cheese or frozen pancakes. Raw hot dogs are Molly's favorite, oddly. She grabs them out of the fridge and sits on the floor to eat. Going for her first bite excited to eat something . . .

"Molly!" her mother yells as she comes down the stairs.

Jen hurries into the kitchen to find Molly eating on the floor.

"We have to go. Come on." she gets closer to Molly.

Molly feels another jerk in her gut, her gut urging and throbbing in caution.

"What? What's going on?" Molly questions while getting up. She couldn't even take a second bight before she had to get up.

"I'll tell you later. Come on let's go."

Jen pulls Molly by the hand as she bolts up the stairs. Molly stumbling and trying to keep up as she looks back at her food and feels a rumble in her tummy. She could feel the fear and pain radiate off of her mother's body. The fear has now transferred to Molly. Jen never lets Molly see her fear, but this, this is different. Something is seriously wrong, but what? What could be so horrible when *he* isn't even around?

"Mom, what's going on?" she asks as they run into her mother's room, closing and locking the door behind them.

"Just trust me. Ok?" her mother says while looking Molly deep into her eyes.

*Trust her? How can I do that when I don't know what's going on?* She wonders. *What could be so horribly wrong, and how could it make my mom so scared?*

A bang comes from downstairs. Footsteps enter the house and vibrate under Molly's tiny toes. Her entire body tenses up and goosebumps spike across the surface of her skin, creating a chill.

"Molly hurry! Help me move the bed!" her mother says, her voice rattling in fear.

Footsteps start up the stairs and the old house creeks with every step. Echos' pound throughout the house, it's hard to make out what the person is saying, even hard to tell who it is.

"Jen! Where are you! Don't make me find you. Believe me, it'll be a lot worse if I have to come find you!" the voice says in an intense aggressive tone, causing the entire house to tremble at its structure.

The voice sounds all too familiar, it's Noc.

Molly helps her mother move the bed without hesitation. They push the bed sideways then slide it up against the door blocking it from opening inward. Noc pounds on the door, as if he is using every muscle in his body just to make a statement. The doorknob twists as he tries to enter, making more than just a statement.

"I know you're in there Jen!" Noc says with deadly aggression.

He continues to pound on the door and screams to Jen through the wall. The house rattles from the screaming and beating upon its walls. Molly can't seem to focus on the words that are being transferred between them, she can only focus on the fear and worries that make her entire body weak.

*What if he gets in? What if the door breaks down and he takes his anger out on my mom? Or me?* The worries override her mind. *What if this time he has so much anger he won't know when to stop, and kills her? What then. . ?*

"Come on honey. Come on out. I won't hurt you." Noc says, this time in a calm persuading voice.

Jen's body trembles, her face wet with tears. Her body looking even weaker than this morning.

"Go away Noc, or I will call the police." her mother yells out to him. Her body shaking weakly as if she could fold at any moment. But she won't let herself, she needs to protect Molly. How could she protect Molly when her own body is on the verge of collapsing?

"Come on hun I won't hurt you, please come out." Noc is now begging.

Jen slightly gives in, she walks toward the bed in hesitation to move it aside.

"Mom no!" Molly runs to her mother's side. "Please don't open the door," she begs.

She tries so hard to keep the tears in and to do her very best to stay strong. She has to be strong so that she can protect her mother. Her mother is too weak to confront him, no matter how innocent he wants to act Molly knows he isn't anywhere near innocent.

"Jen I'm sorry!" Noc's voice escalates.

Jen walks towards the bed and starts to move it.

"Mom!" Molly screams, grabbing onto her mother's hand. "Please don't open the door . . . please," she begs into her mother's eyes for the second time.

Jen looks Molly straight in the eye, then back to the door. Jen hesitates . . . then continues to move the bed. Molly drops to her knees and lets the tears flood down her cheeks creating a puddle down by her knees.

*Why is my voice not enough? Does she even hear me speak? Am I invisible?* Molly thinks helplessly. *Or am I just not enough?*

Jen moves the bed aside and reaches for the deadbolt . . .

"Jen! Open the damn door!" Noc yells at the top of his lungs.

Her mother jumps back and tumbles onto the bed. Jen sits there blank-faced. Thudding vibrates along the walls, making the wall art shake. Jen gathers herself and stands.

"Go away Noc!" Jen yells back through the wall.

"No! If you don't come out here I will come in there!" Noc yells back in a threatening tone.

"I'm calling the police."

Jen grabs her phone and dials 911. She reports to them what is happening. Footsteps start down the stairs and out of the house.

Molly feels relief glide throughout her body. She wipes her tears aside and dries her wet hands off on her pants. She runs over and hugs her mother, feeling warmth fill her cheeks. Jen kisses Molly on the head and pulls her in closer. Her mother's body trembles against her own, along with their pounding hearts.

Sirens sound down the street and make their way closer. A sudden knock hits the downstairs door . . .

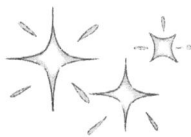

## Chapter 3

# Friendly Strangers

The knocking gradually gets louder. Jen unlocks the door and hurries down the stairs. Molly follows close behind.

"Molly stay here." her mother says while gesturing for her to stay.

"But mom . . ." she manages to let out.

"I'll be fine. Stay here."

Molly stays, in fear she won't be able to protect her mother in the time of something happening. She peeks her head around the corner s0 she can keep a lookout and make sure her mother will be alright.

Jen opens the door, flashing lights enter into the house.

*Why are there such bright flashing lights?* Molly wonders.

"Hello, officers." her mother says to the two men standing at the door.

"Afternoon ma'am." an officer says.

"Come in."

The two officers step foot into the house and continue talking to Jen. Molly can't understand what they are saying, she's too far away. She runs up behind her mother's back and grabs onto Jen's arm.

"Where is he now?" the officer carries on with the conversation.

"I . . . he didn't say where he was going he just left." her mother continues.

"Well, what are we supposed to do . . . ?"

She looks up, scanning the officer's tall and slim body. They are extremely tall, yet they look close to her mother's height. Maybe Molly is just really small?

Molly zones out and starts dwelling on what Noc could have done. How badly he could have hurt her mother, or herself. He surely could have done real permanent damage to either of them. With all the anger he had, he wouldn't have known when to quit.

"Ok thanks officers," Jen says sarcastically.

"Have a good night ma'am." the officers say as they leave the house.

*Where are they going, aren't they supposed to help us?* Molly thinks as she watches the officers disappear into their cop car.

"Mom, why are they leaving?" she asks.

"They're not going to help us." her mother says painfully. "We'll be fine."

Molly can't understand why they won't help. Isn't that what their job is? Aren't they supposed to protect people?

*Maybe this all is normal and we overreacted,* Molly thinks. *Maybe I overreacted.*

Jen locks the main door and heads up into her room. Molly stands there, alone, and afraid.

. . .

Molly and her mother both fell asleep alone and scared last night. No words were exchanged between the two of them, only cries overheard through the walls. Although yesterday was difficult and dreadfully frightening, it is a new day and Molly hopes it will be better than yesterday.

She crawls out of her bed and drags her feet along into the bathroom where she wipes her eye crusties away from the rough night sleep. Her mother's scream had somehow made it into her dreams last night, making Molly feel even more helpless.

Stepping onto her step stool, she looks into the mirror and sees her bright hazel eyes look back at her, her eyes redden as she feels the pain sink into the pit of her stomach. A slight rub over her belly does nothing, the pain refuses to wane. It embeds itself throughout her body releasing an ache everywhere. Molly steps away from the mirror and walks herself over to her window to watch the grey fluffy clouds overhead.

Watching the clouds gives Molly a chance to create her own dreams and imagine whatever she desires. At night she dreams upon nightmares unwillingly, it's impossible for her to escape the deep and tense dreams. The clouds give her a chance to be in control and create her own outcome. Day after day Molly dreams of becoming someone big, important, and inspiring. No matter what she becomes well known for, she wants to inspire people, she wants to impact lives. Changing lives is the start of changing the world.

*I see a dragon in that cloud.* Molly's mind wanders off into the fluffy shapes that fill the sky. *Oh, I see a tiger, though it doesn't look all that scary, he looks kind and harmless. . .*

Before she can finish the thought she hears her mother's alarm go off. The same alarm that plays practically every day, instead of a continuous beeping it is a song. Molly happens to like the song, though she can not tell what song it is. She walks down the hall and into her mother's room. Goosebumps ride up her arms, in fear of him being in there. She peaks her head into the room and only sees her mom, goosebumps settle slightly, leaving a chill.

The alarm gets louder as Molly walks deeper into the room. She sees the phone and fiddles with it, in an attempt to find an off button. More fiddling goes on but no luck is found. Her mom hasn't made a single movement since Molly has entered the room. She finally turns the alarm off and begins the struggle of trying to wake her mother. A suttle tap at first then progressing into a rough nudge, still no movement from her mom.

"Mom. Wake up. Mom?" she says. "Come on you're scaring me . . . please be ok."

Jen moves her leg into a stretching position. Molly continues to nudge upon her mother's arm.

~ *Passion From Within* ~

"Mom get up," she says, beginning to nudge harder.

Jen finally rolls over and opens her emerald green eyes, looking Molly directly in the eyes while rubbing away the crust beneath her lashes. Molly feels her goosebumps go away as she makes eye contact with her mom.

Jen's shiny red-tinted hair lays along the bed, her fair skin glistening from the shining sunlight. The bruises from yesterday still spread across her body.

"Morning sweetheart," Jen says.

"Goodmorning," Molly replies as she looks into her mother's shining eyes.

"I have a surprise for you today." her mother says weekly while stroking Molly's hair.

"Really? What is it?" she asks, being ever so curious.

"If I told you, it wouldn't be much of a surprise," Jen says with a widespread grin.

Molly smiles as she thinks about what the surprise could be. Today already has a better start than yesterday and that gives her a step towards what she had hoped for this morning.

"Go get ready, we'll leave, shortly," her mother says, as she gets up out of bed.

"Ok," Molly replies.

She runs down the hallway full of excitement for what the day will bring. She slides into her best outfit and waits for her mom to come to do her hair.

Rain starts to travel down Molly's window. She watches the water droplets race down the glass, trying to guess which droplet will reach the bottom of the window first. The droplets glide along the window panel leaving a watery trail in its tracks. A smell of wet sidewalk fills into her room along with a slight chill. The window is still slightly cracked from just a few days ago.

"Molly?" Jen says while walking into Molly's room.

"Yeah?" Molly replies.

"Let's get your hair done quickly, we have to go soon." her mother parts her hair into two sections and tightens them into pigtails. "Alright, turn around."

She turns and faces her mother.

"Beautiful." her mother examines her reddish-brown hair. "Alright, let's get going we have to be there shortly. Are you ready?"

"Yeah . . . ready as I'll ever be," she says while walking away from the racing raindrops.

They get into the car and breathe in the musty smell of tobacco. She watches raindrops into the puddles as they drive along the highway. Watching the ripples create and flow to the edges. Nerves fill her stomach and her head, she takes a deep breath to clear her thoughts. The clouds are too grey to create an imaginative image, but that doesn't stop Molly from the passionate dreaming. She lays her head against the window, watching her dreams form upon the clouds grey canvas.

Curiosity sparks in Molly. She wants to know where they are going, or what they are doing, and why. She is completely clueless. They're driving all the way across town for whatever it is. What could it be?

"Are you excited?" her mother asks.

"Yes, but I still don't know what the surprise could be?" she says while questioning the scenery.

"I'll tell you when we get there."

Molly rests her head upon her hand and looks up into the sky continuing to dream.

. . .

After a while of driving, Molly looks up and sees a playground. A colorful playground is full of wet woodchips and no kids.

"Why are we here?" she asks. They live right across the street from a playground. Why did they drive so far just to play at a different one?

"You're here to meet your dad," Jen says. "I brought your bike so you can bike around. You are going to spend the afternoon with him. You're not allowed to leave the park, and I will come back in a little while."

"What?" she asks in total confusion. "I thought I already have a dad? "

"He isn't your biological dad. This guy is."

"What's his name?"

"Dollan."

"Ok . . . I don't want to meet him, I already have a dad. Sam, he is my dad."

*I don't want to call this stranger dad. I already have a dad.* Molly's thoughts are flying everywhere from the abrupt news.

"I will come with you ok? He is already here."

"No. I have a dad."

~ Riley Brett ~

"Come on, please just try. For me, ok?"

". . .Fine, only for you."

They get out of the car, their feet soaked with rainwater. Molly gets onto her bike and sits there dwelling on her thoughts.

*Real dad? What does that mean?* She wonders. She pushes her thoughts aside and proceeds by her mother's side.

They approach a man sitting on a concrete slab; Brown short thin hair peeking out from under his hat, slightly faded jeans, and a freshly cleaned t-shirt, and a smell of tobacco and alcohol surround him. Molly continues to look down at her shoes, staying loyal to her *real* dad.

"Hi, I . . . I'm your dad," Dollan says.

"No, you're not," Molly says in rejection. He can't be, she grew up with a dad, Sam. And this man, this man is not her dad.

"Molly, remember what we talked about." her mother says, scowling her comment.

"Sorry."

*He isn't, I feel bad but it's true.* Molly thinks. *I'll try to be nicer I guess.*

"I like your bike," Dollan says.

"Thanks," she replies.

*If he really is my dad, why does he feel like a stranger?* She wonders.

"Alright well, I'll let you guys get to know each other. Call me if you need anything, I will only be a few blocks away." her mother says.

"Mom," she says, trying to hold back the tears.

"You'll be fine sweety, I love you."

"Love you too," she replies, her throat tightening as she watches her mother drive away, fighting the temptation to run after her mother.

"It's ok, we'll have fun," Dollan says with a semi-forced smile.

". . .ok." she manages to say.

Molly drives her bike around in circles trying to ease her mind. Despite being strong and brave she can be very shy, even with her "dad".

Minutes full of awkward silence go by feeling like hours. Still no sign of anyone saying anything. What are you supposed to say to your "dad" you just met?

"So do you like to fish?" Dollan asks.

"Yeah, my grandpa takes me fishing up at our cabin," Molly replies with a little smile, remembering all the amazing memories that have been created up at their family's cabin with her grandparents.

"Right on. Maybe we could fish sometime?"

"Mhm," Molly says. She is getting more comfortable as the conversation goes on, but he is still a stranger. Making plans with him, even if he is a friendly stranger makes her feel uncomfortable.

"What about agates? You like those?" Dollan asks.

"What are agates?" Molly replies.

"You don't know what agates are? What do you live under a rock?" Dollan asks, laughing at his "dad joke". How ironic.

"No I don't think so," she answers. It was a stupid joke, but she let out a giggle anyway.

*Live under a rock? Is that even possible?* She wonders.

"They are really cool looking rocks. Most of the time they are colorful, but not always. Sometimes they can even look like an ordinary rock and on the inside be a colorful agate." Dollan replies with his inner excitement coming out.

"Wow, that sounds nice," she says. "So I have a question."

"Go ahead."

"If you're my dad, how come I am meeting you now?" she asks. "I have a dad already, how can I have two?"

"Good questions. I will tell you more when you are older. As for now, I am sorry I haven't been around, but I want to make it up to you. We will have so much fun together. We can pick agates, fish, camp, and spend holidays together. . .what I am trying to say is all that matters is that I am here now and I will try to make up for the lost time." Dollan explains.

It is still confusing to Molly, but what Dollan said makes it somewhat easier to understand. *Maybe* she can trust him after all.

"Ok. I still don't know what agates are." she giggles.

"I'll tell you what, why don't we drive by my house and take a look at some. We'll be quick and we can pick some candy up on the way there."

"Yeah, that sounds great," she says with excitement.

"You can't tell your mom though. It'll be our little secret." Dollan says.

"Ok . . ." she hesitates. It should be fine because after all, it is her dad, right? But her mom specifically said not to leave the park.

"I need a car seat," she says, looking at the front seat hesitant.

"It will be fine, I will drive extra slow and careful," Dollan replies, gesturing for her to get into the car.

Molly hops onto the passenger seat as Dollan puts her bike in the back. Instantly she inhales strong sent of tobacco causing her to cough. The car has clean floors and objects arranged perfectly, all besides the ashtray which lays in the crevices of the front counsel.

Along the road, leaves fly around creating patches of swirling colors. The sky is brightening up causing the blue sky to peek through the dark grey clouds. Molly feels her gut ache as she thinks about how she will lie to her mother, she pushes the thought aside before regret can cloud her mind.

"What kind of candy would you like?" Dollan asks as they pull into the gas station parking lot.

". . .gummies, please," she says.

He shuts the door and runs inside. Molly sits there alone in a car reeking of cigarettes and alcohol. She looks throughout the car and feels regret flood her mind.

*She specifically told me not to leave. . . she also told me to try and get along with him. It should be fine.* She tries to ease her conscience.

Looking out the window she sees the blue skies fill with large fluffy clouds, perfect for imagining. She lays her head along with the window and lets her imagination wander upon the bright blue skies. The sky makes her feel free, free from all the worries and troubles. It's the perfect escape.

Dollan opens the car door and hands Molly the package of gummies. She opens it right up and chews away.

"Ready?" Dollan asks.

"Yep." she replies with her mouth stuffed with gummies.

Along the long highway, she watches all the cars driving by. All the colorful cars, there are so many colors. Molly lets her mind wander again while chewing her gummies.

Minutes have passed before she knows it they are crossing the bridge into a whole other state.

"Where are we going?" she asks, slightly frightened.

"Don't worry it's just up the road from the bridge," Dollan says.

Molly is frightened by how far they are going. She just met this man about 30 minutes ago. What if this isn't even her dad and he is just pretending? Her mother would never do that to her. Or would she?

They continue driving a few more minutes. Eventually reaching a road that is edged with bright green grass. The grass is so bright and healthy-looking, Molly has never seen anything like it. Her gaze stays upon the grass, even when the grass cuts off. Everything is so lively and well taken care of, the scenery is comforting. She loses track of where they are going.

The car comes to a stop, and right in front of them is a wooden tall house. Cut in the middle creating a top and bottom duplex. The wood is stressed and soaked with rainwater. There is a swing set in the yard, looking fairly new.

"Here. I did forget to mention, I have a roommate. Her name is Kimberly, we call her Kimmy though." Dollan says while getting out of the car.

*Her??* She thinks, emphasizing the fact that it is a girl.

"Ok," she replies.

"Follow me," Dollan says as he walks up the stairs.

Molly follows him up the rickety steps. Breathing in the smell of freshly cut grass. They walk into his half of the duplex and are greeted by a few cats. One after another, they keep popping up. There are so many cats, how many could there be?

"Hello." a girl says with a smile. "I'm Kimmy."

"Hi" she manages to say while forcing a smile. This is a little much, meeting your dad for the first time who is a *stranger* and his roommate who is a woman. Did he leave her mother for this woman? Did he leave Molly for this woman?

"Come on in. I'll go get those agates for you to look at." Dollan says.

"Ok," she replies while stepping foot into the dim apartment.

There are so many cats. Strong sent of cat litter and tobacco come from all around Molly. She tries not to breathe any of it in, but that's impossible when you are standing in a house that contains so many cats. A chill of discomfort settles itself upon her skin. After all, she is in a stranger's house.

"Here they are. You can go ahead and look through them." Dollan says while walking in with a huge container of agates.

"Kimmy and I picked most of them together." a big smile spreads across his face.

*Oh great. Why do I dislike her so much?* Molly wonders.

"Wow these are cool . . ." she says, trying her best to look interested.

"I know right! Look at all these big ones. I hope we can pick agates together someday. Then I can make an agate lamp with them! Wouldn't that be cool?" Dollan replies, somehow his smile gets even bigger.

"Yeah, that sounds fun," she says, hope fills her mind.

"Right on. We should probably get going so that your mom doesn't wonder where you are." Dollan says. He sets the large container of agates down on a table.

"It was nice meeting you," Kimberly says.

"Nice meeting you too," Molly replies.

They walk out of Dollan's apartment and make their way down the steps. Molly feels so weird. Looking at the playset in his yard. A spark of jealousy flares within her. If he *really* is her dad then she should be able to use that playset. Why would he even have a playset if she didn't even know he existed?

"Is that your playset?" she asks.

"No, it's the downstairs neighbor's" Dollan replies, while unlocking his car door.

"Oh." an odd feeling of relief fills her body.

They get in the car and drive over to the spot they met, in hopes that they can get back before Jen arrives.

Confusion wanders around Molly's head, so many questions forming; If this is really her dad then why doesn't he feel like it? How come he feels like a complete stranger? He's a friendly stranger but still a stranger, someone that is completely unknown. Why has it taken so long for them to meet? And how come she doesn't live with him if that is truly her father?

Before she can finish forming more questions, they pull into the parking lot of the playground. To the side of Dollan's car, there is a dark green 4 runner . . . the exact kind that Jen drives.

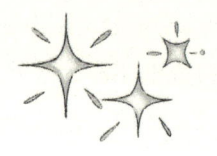

## Chapter 4

# Pushing Point

Dark tinted windows reflect Molly's face back at her. The windows are too dark to tell who's inside of the vehicle. Getting closer she realizes there is nobody in the truck. Molly lets out a sigh of relief, as she turns around she sees her mother's truck pull into the parking lot. Instantly tensing back up. How could she lie to her mother? Lying is one of her weaknesses. A forced smile spreads across her face as she makes eye contact with her mom, instant nerves flow through her body.

Her mother pulls her car aside from Molly.

"You ready?" Jen asks.

"Yeah," she replies, trying to keep ahold of the secret.

"Bye Molly. We'll have to get together soon and go fishing or something." Dollan says.

~ *Passion From Within* ~

"Yeah for sure. Nice meeting you," she says with a smile.

They pull out of the parking lot and head back to her mom's house. The sky is now a steady clear blue. Clear blue skies are rare in the country of Votum, weather here consists mostly of; rain, clouds, and chilly or cold weather. It's nice to see blue skies for a change.

"How was it?" her mother asks.

"It was fine," she responds.

A moment of silence goes by and butterflies fill her stomach.

"Good," Jen says.

Molly pushes her secret aside and begins to think about how much fun her *dad* said they'd have together. Imagine all the fishing she'll do, all the Walleyes' she will catch and the colorful rocks they'll pick. Molly and her grandfather love to catch walleye, though she holds the record for the most caught on a boating trip. Along with the longest. She'll surely surprise her *dad* with how well she can fish. Images pop up into Molly's head almost creating a trailer as to what the future holds . . .

*Kids' play around a lake with fishing poles held in pole holders along the dock, just waiting for the perfect fish to come along and nibble on their bate. The sun setting upon the shimmery blue lake, creating an orange and pink sunset. Frogs hopping from puddle to puddle from last night's rain, trying to catch the flies buzzing in the afternoon breeze. When it gets dark enough the stars will glow with hopeful glimmer, just as everyone looks up upon the sky a shooting star crosses and everyone hopes for a day just as amazing as the present one. Before everyone gathers in for the nightly fire, fireflies appear at the edge of the woods. Their tiny lights flickering throughout the trees creating a night light for adventurers' who behold an itching curiosity. Breathing in the smokey smell of the fire they will share the last few flickering flames by making s' mores' and enjoying every last crumb as they fall upon the ground's damp dirt. Lastly, everyone will snuggle into the colorful tents, sharing the spookiest story their imagination can bring. Flashlights creating multiple shadow puppet images to go along with the stories from each child. As everyone reaches exhaustion they turn out the lanterns and fall asleep to the crickets late-night chirp.*

As they pull onto their driveway's crooked bricks, Molly's daydream comes to an end. So much hope has been brought to her and she is enjoying every last bit of it.

*This could be the end. The end to all the beating on mom's body. He could save us.* She thinks with a huge smile spreading from one rosy cheek to the other, *their savior.*

She runs inside full of excitement. Apart from all the hope, an outfit needs to be picked out for tomorrow, her 5th birthday. Running into her closet she finds a comfortable dress and tights to go with it. The dress is yellow with white lace and pink flowers covering the bottom, with white tights to go along with it. Her shoes are all white with buckle straps over the top. She prepares each piece of the outfit out on the dresser for the morning.

Molly gathers toys' from her toybox and aligns them for a game. All her stuffies being set up in a line behind the smaller plastic toys. Stuffies are the guardians of any game she plays. They sit along the top of tall stacked objects, ready to come into play whenever a bad guy comes through creating a ruckus. Most of the stuffies are large-bodied with big round eyes. She trusts that their big eyes will catch any trouble inside her imaginary town.

"Hey, sweetie. You excited for tomorrow?" her mother asks while she enters Molly's room.

"Yes! I can't wait." she responds,". . .I have a question."

"What is it?"

"Will Dollan be there?" a little smile weaves its way across her face.

"Yes, he said he will be there."

"Ok." her smile gradually gets bigger. So much excitement running throughout her mind. Continuing to play with her toys she thinks about how much fun she'll have tomorrow.

Jen cracks the door shut as she leaves the room. Molly is deep in her imaginary toy town, now there is a villain in her town trying to destroy all the buildings'. Salvus comes running in and knocks over the entire town. The cat runs over to Molly and lays along her side.

"Salvus? What's wrong?" she asks while looking down at Salvus.

Footsteps creek down the hallway quickly shifting towards the stairs.

"Please . . . please not today." her mother pleads.

"You don't get a say in what happens to you. Your voice is useless!" Noc says. His words rattling throughout Molly's body.

Molly focuses her eyes on what is happening just outside her door.

Jen backs up closer and closer to the stair's edge. Noc closes her in knowing the outcome. He aggressively grabs upon her fragile body and grips with all of his strength.

Molly tiptoes closer to her door and peeks through the doors crack. Watching every step. Every touch. Every sob. Hearing the deadly aggression within Noc's voice. All the pain travels throughout Molly's body as she watches her mother squirm. All creating a forever scar.

The intense suspense fills Molly's arms as she grips herself into a hug, trying to comfort the frightening chills. Her heart races as she watches her mother cry. He harms her in every way possible, giving no way to escape it.

His fingers grip along her mother's weak arms, until he loosens his grip, and pushes . . . Jen's body skims along the creaking stairs as she tumbles all the way down.

"Mom!" she screams.

"Moll go to bed," Noc says while slamming Molly's bedroom door shut, centimeters away from her nose. She can feel the breeze from the door brush along her frightened skin.

"No!" Molly yells while pounding along the door. "Leave her alone! Please . . . please." her knees give in and her body tumbles to the floor. Laying along her bedroom hardwood floors, the trembles take over every inch of her body. Tears begin down her warm cheeks. No voice, he did that to her. He took it from her as if it was an object he could take whenever he wants.

The floor shakes all along its floorboards. Noc's muffled voice echoing throughout the house.

*No. He'll kill her . . . easily. She's too weak, and her body is already so full of bruises. He'll surely do it.* Worries fill her mind, and sobs weep from her tightened throat. *Please . . . please, she can't die. She's my mom and I need her.*

Molly forces herself up, every limb shakes as she forces them to move. Putting her hand on the door she feels the fear. All kinds of fear. She pushes it all aside and she opens her door, his voice becoming more clear.

*Please leave her alone.* She wishes.

Worries crowd her mind and make it hard to think of the right thing to do. She shakes her head and takes a deep breath. None of her fears matter right now, all that matters is that she has a voice and she needs to use it. No matter how much Noc wants to try and mute it, it's there.

Molly tiptoes down the stairs trying not to make a sound. All of the spy games that she has played with her friends are starting to come in handy. Clashing slowly decreases. Peeking her head around the wall she sees her mother laying on the floor and Noc sitting on top of her. Molly sits on the stair step below her feet, she sits there trying to think of what to do. It's difficult to think when your mind is blurred by doubt and fear.

Noc gets up off of Jen and looks over by Molly. Molly quickly looks away and hides behind the wall. . .

Footsteps creak across the room after moments go by the front door opens and slams. Molly looks over and he's gone, Noc left. Jen's body lays along the floor with no movement.

"Mom?" she says, running over to her mother. "Mom . . . you're ok." Molly fights all the tears stinging her eyes. Her body shakes and trembles at *the* thought.

*No. She's fine. She just needs some rest. . . she's tired.* She tries to convince herself.

Her body shaking with *the* thought. Cries build up behind her soar eyes.

"Mom . . . please be ok. . . please." she falls to the side of her mother, whimpering sobs release from all throughout her body.

Jen lays along the carpet. Her body bruised and cut up. How could her body look even more fragile than yesterday? Her pale skin turned black and blue, her fair-skinned face turned red and bloody. *Her*, unlively and ever so vulnerable.

Molly stays in the presence of her mother, praying to God she'll be ok. . .

Moments later Jen moves and gradually tries to sit up.

"Mom . . . are you ok?" she asks.

"I'm fine sweetie . . . I just . . . I'm clumsy and I tripped. That's all." her mother says weakly, beginning to stand.

Jen wobbles, slowly trying to keep still. She looks Molly in the eye, "I'm fine, it's just a scrape." her mother assures her.

Molly hugs her mom, "Ok. Please be more careful." she says.

*I must have overreacted again . . . but I watched him push her. Maybe he was trying to catch her?* She thinks, trying to understand what had just happened.

All kinds of questions form in Molly's head. It's hard to tell what's normal in the world when you have yet to experience it for yourself. All you can do is go off of what others tell you, that is particularly hard when you don't know if you can trust them. Being so young with so little experience makes it so much more confusing and makes all the bad things feel oddly normal. Until one day you realize, "normal" doesn't exist, but safety and comfort do.

Molly walks into the kitchen to grab a glass of water for her mom. While she gets the water she questions her mom's comment.

*Clumsy? That was the second time this month. Even if she fell because of him, there isn't anything I can do, I fear just speaking around him, there is no way I could stand up to him.* Her thoughts try to sort themselves.

Walking back into the living room, Molly hands her mom a glass of water.

"Thank you," Jen says.

Molly smiles back at Jen. She smiles in hope of it passing on to her mother, possibly making her happier. It always seems to help Molly when she is in pain, smiling keeps her in a positive place. Gradually reaching for genuine happiness.

"It's getting late. Go get ready for bed, you have a big day tomorrow." her mother says, swallowing a sip of water.

"Ok. Are you going to be alright?" she asks.

"I will be fine. Now go get ready for bed."

Molly slowly heads up the stairs, the stairs her mom had just tumbled down. The images keep popping up in her head, along with the sound of her mother's body hitting each rickety stair.

## ~ Riley Brett ~

She doesn't understand why she cannot stop thinking about it, or why it keeps popping up so vividly. After all her mother said she'd tripped because of her clumsiness. Normal, right?

Sitting on her bed she tries to take everything in from what had just happened. Still, images and sounds keep showing up in her head like a slideshow. She wonders why the images will not leave her be and how she can stop the echoing sound of her mother's falling body. A sting behind her eyes begins as she lays down along her bedding. Tears threaten her eyes while she thinks of all the fear that her body held today.

*It was too close this time. I need to speak up for her. She doesn't deserve this. Maybe turning 5 tomorrow could change things, maybe I will be strong enough to talk. I hope I will be strong enough.* She tries to comfort her young struggling mind.

Tears' build up in her eyes. Tear by tear they begin down her warm face. Cries come from her body, all the built-up pain tries to make its way out of her. . .

*Molly hears objects breaking throughout the house. Screams being let out and intensified by each clash. She stands alone in her dark empty room, all her objects are gone. They have vanished. The room is dark and lonely, it is only herself and her inner thoughts.*

*She looks around the room, trying to figure out what is happening. The only light is the street lights shining in from her window, creating a dim striped track across her floor.*

*More cries echo through her walls. A scream makes its way out of her body, but it makes no sound. She tries to scream again but nothing comes out. Her voice is gone. Completely taken. No means* of communication, just her vulnerable trembling body. More yells and screams come from the other side of her bedroom walls. She wonders if it is her mother who is screaming.

She moves over to her door and tries to the best of her ability to open it . . . but it won't budge. It's locked. Molly is trapped. No voice. No exit. No light, just her vulnerability.

Screams continue to fight their way out of her body, but again, no sound. She has officially been muted.

She beats upon her rickety door, her fists pounding and pounding as hard as she can possibly hit. The door rattles but doesn't give in to her weak beating. Her arms and legs become sore, aching, and pleading for a break.

Her body falls like a teardrop, and lays on the floor; scared, confused, and alone. . .

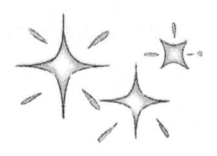

## Chapter 5

# A Party To Remember

Molly opens her damp eyes to the bright sunlight shining onto her face. Her body shaking from the intense nightmare that had locked her in a deep scary night's sleep. It had felt so real. She is having trouble believing that it didn't actually happen. The way that her voice had been muted. Is that a possibility? Can her voice be taken, permanently?

She tries not to think about the nightmare because it's a big day. It's her birthday! She forgets about all the troubling thoughts. It's another rare sunny day. Blue skies and white fluffy clouds. She sits by her window and looks up into the clouds. While looking into the fluffy shapes she thinks about all of her friends that will be there. Most importantly she thinks about her Nana and Papa being there. They are Molly's favorite people in the entire world, not many can compare.

"Happy birthday!" her mother says while walking in with an in-bed breakfast. She sets the food down onto Molly's bed.

Molly smiles from ear to ear. "Thank you!" she says.

"Are you excited?" Jen asks.

"Yes. I can't wait to see my friends and Dollan again."

Jen smiles as she looks into Molly's eyes and feels her excitement radiate throughout the room. Their hands grip together and comfort each other's worries.

"Enjoy your breakfast then get ready for your party. We'll be leaving shortly." her mother says as she exits the room.

Molly digs into her delightful looking waffles and enjoys every bit of it, down to the last powdered sugar crumb.

She sets the tray aside and proceeds to put her birthday outfit on. The skies are bright and the day's hope is strong. Not much can go wrong when you're this happy, nothing can change this happiness.

Her mom comes into her room to do her hair. Her mother brushes along Molly's thick blonde hair and puts it into pig tales. Both of the little ponytails have two beads along its loop. They always seem to get caught in Molly's hair and become a huge mess, her hair gets snarly and it takes about 5 minutes to get the beads untangled from her hair. But they are always used for special occasions, despite the time-consuming mess.

"There. They look adorable" Jen says with a vibrant smile.

"Thank you!" Molly replies.

"Give me a few minutes, then we can go to the hotel and get the room ready for the party." Jen gets up and leaves the room.

Molly wanders off to her window and gazes into the shapes filling the bright blue sky. So much hope being built up for the day to come. Its imminence is making her impatient. The thought of seeing Dollan again makes her happy. She's already missed out on years with him, she can't wait to get to know him better and go on all the adventures he said they'd go on.

"Molly, let's go," Jen yells from downstairs.

She quickly grabs her shoes and says goodbye to Salvus on the way out of her bedroom. Running down the stairs and into the kitchen she sees all the party items her mother has gathered. All the balloons make her heart warm with excitement.

She follows her mom out of the house and down the sidewalk to their car.

"Hold on." her mother says while holding Molly back from getting into the car . . .

"What? What's wrong?" she asks.

"Nothing, it's fine. Just stay there"

Molly walks closer to the car, the driver's window is shattered and a brick is on the driver's seat. There's a note on it. . . but she can't get close enough to read what the note says.

"Stand back. It's fine I'll figure it out." Jen says as she pulls Molly back. "I'll just have Nana come pick us up." Jen grabs the note and stuffs it into her pocket.

Molly steps aside and sits on their driveway's lopsided bricks. Jen calls her mom in hopes she can drive them to the hotel.

"Hey . . . are you in town yet?" Jen speaks into her phone while walking away from Molly.

*~ Passion From Within ~*

Molly's grandparents live a few hours north of Orsus, the town she has been growing up in. They live on a nice property with a small lake view and trails all around their home leading deep into the woods that surround them. In the center of a town called Solatium.

Her mother comes walking back towards the car.

"Is she coming?" Molly asks.

"Yes. She'll be here in 5 minutes." her mother responds.

"Yay! Is Papa coming too?"

"No, he had to finish up some work at his office, he'll try to make it in the morning."

"Oh, ok." her smile weakens.

They walk around to the front and wait for Jen's mom to come. Molly feels disappointment hit her as she thinks about her Papa. She misses him. He has always been the one person she aspires to be like the most. She looks up to everything he does, even when he makes mistakes, to her they don't seem like true mistakes because he makes them seem so perfect, as if he meant to do it. He learns from his mistakes, knowing he doesn't know everything there is to know, and that he never will, but he can try.

A car pulls up aside from the curb and rolls down their window.

"Come on we're going to be late." her Nana says.

"Let's go, Molly," Jen repeats to Molly.

She springs onto her feet and into the car. They drive past the speed limit in order to get to the hotel on time.

Arriving in the parking lot they see one of Molly's friends'.

"Mom look it's Amity!" Molly says while putting her hand on the door handle.

"Hold on, wait for the car to stop," Jen replies.

Amity is Molly's very best friend. Their moms were in rehab together about a year ago. Molly met Amity during one of the visits to her mom's rehab center. Ever since then they've been really good friends.

As soon as the car comes to a complete stop Molly opens the door and runs over to Amity. They greet each other with a tight hug.

"Happy birthday!" Amity says.

"Thank you!" Molly replies.

"We're finally the same age. Took you long enough . . ." Amity giggles.

Molly laughs along with Amity. They are about three months apart in age, and Amity loves to remind Molly that she's older, even if it is *only* three months.

"Here's your gift." Amity hands Molly a colorful bag with tissue paper sticking out.

"Thank you!" Molly replies. "Mom look!"

"Wow, that was nice of Amity to get you a gift. Let's go set the room up, then you guys can put your suits on and go swimming. How's that sound?" Jen asks.

"Ok!"

"I'll come get you tomorrow. Have fun, I love you." Amity's mom says.

"I love you too," Amity replies.

As soon as Amity's mom pulls away they all walk into the hotel and get the room keys. With a cart full of bags and party supplies Molly is feeling very happy and excited. They get into an elevator and out into a long hallway until they make it to their room, opening it up they see this big beautiful space. There's bunk beds, two queen size beds, two TVs, and a large table. It is beyond perfect.

Molly runs in and plops on the queen bed closest to them. Looking up at the ceiling she feels happiness fill her cheeks and slowly fill the rest of her body. She's safe. She's happy. She's comfortable. Even if it's all just for one day, she is thankful for the relieving rest.

Amity giggles and hops onto the bed right next to Molly. They lay there and appreciate the comfortable bed beneath them.

"Molly. Liz and Camry are here, can you guys go to the lobby and get them." Jen says.

"Yeah," Molly replies as Amity and her run out of the room and up the hotel stairs.

Giggles come from the two girls as they race up the staircase. Molly tries the best she can to get to the top first but her giggles are too restrictive.

"I won!" Amity shouts.

"Yeah whatever. . ." Molly replies with here inner competitivity coming out.

They giggle even more as they enter the lobby. There they see Molly's two friends.

"Hey! Happy birthday Molly." Liz and Camry say almost in unison.

They're her friends from preschool. Liz and Molly always spend the morning time at school making little art projects out of plastic beads. Liz is unbelievably good at making art, Molly struggles to keep up with Liz's creativity. Camry plays kitchen with Molly during lunch. They are always the last two kids done with lunch, though it works well because they have each other to play with.

"Thank you," Molly says with a giggle spilling out.

Amity giggles along with Molly.

"Bye mom, love you," Camry says to her mother.

"See you tomorrow, love you too." Camry's mom replies while hugging her.

Liz tenses up as she watches Camry hug her mom. Her pain is radiating off of her, she looks so sad. Molly wonders what's wrong and why she seems so hurt, by a hug? Molly is confused but doesn't know what to say or what to ask. Instead, she leaves it be and carries on.

"Follow me to the room," Molly says.

Amity walks in front of Molly, practically taunting her with her natural speed. Molly's eager need to win kicks in and she walks past Amity.

"Hey!" Amity says.

"What?" Molly replies while grinning back at Amity.

They begin to race down to the room, leaving Liz and Camry in the dust.

~ *Passion From Within* ~

"I won!" Molly pants out.

Amity giggles, "I let you win. You know, because it's your birthday."

Molly rolls her eyes. The girls walk into the big room, Camry and Liz let out a gasp.

"Woah," Liz says. "There's so much room," she says under her breath, her face filling with sadness.

Molly tilts her head in confusion.

*Something's wrong. But what?* She wonders. *She looks so sad and happy at the same time. . . could she be? Could she be like me? No, because it's normal to be like me. It is normal, isn't it? I'm too scared to ask her. . .*

"Why don't you girls get your suits on and we'll go to the pool?" Jen says.

"Yeah." Molly replies.

"I call changing first," Amity yells out.

*Of course she calls dibs. . .* Molly thinks.

"Ok," Molly replies.

The girls all take their turn changing. Eventually, everyone is ready and Molly's Nana takes them to the pool. They walk down a short hall and quickly reach big doors that open up to a huge colorful waterpark.

Opening the doors all the girls gasp in awe. Finally finding words they speak in unison, "Woah . . ."

They spend hours and hours in the beautiful waterpark. Riding down huge tube slides together and smaller body slides individually in the "kids park". Swirling around the whirlpool.

Even playing water basketball in the large open pool. All that fun taking up so much time yet . . . one question stays in Molly's head. Where is Dollan?

All the girls begin to get tired and need a break from all the tiring fun. They head back to the room and snack on some party foods.

The question continues through her head. She spent her time in the lazy river, in the obstacle course waiting line, and in the hot tub with her eyes locked on the door just waiting for Dollan to come through the doors. She examined every person to step foot through the doors, but he never came.

"Did you girls have fun?" Jen asks.

"Yeah!" everyone replies except for Molly. She is too focused on Dollan, and why he hasn't come yet.

"Molly?" Jen walks towards her.

Molly shakes her head and focuses on the present, "Yeah?"

"You alright?"

"Where is he? He said he'd come." she feels tears pile up behind her eyes, but she holds them in.

"I don't know, he hasn't called. . ." Jen answers, saddened by Molly's disappointment. "You can call him if you want."

"Ok." Molly's hope rises again.

Jen digs through her purse trying to find Dollan's number.

"Found it. Here dial this number into the hotel phone." Jen says.

"Ok." Molly starts to feel nervous, though she can't understand why.

~ *Passion From Within* ~

She picks up the hotel phone and pauses.

*Maybe he just didn't know the party was today. . .* She thinks.

She continues to dial in the number. With every digit, she presses she feels her hand get heavier as if she's making a mistake. The phone rings and rings and rings until finally, it reaches an answering machine, "Hey it's Dollan leave a message. . ."

*He didn't answer.* Her cheeks flush, disappointment fills her mind.

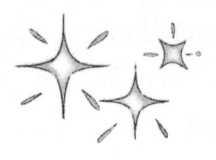

Chapter 6
============

# What He Doesn't Know

"Oh, um hey. It's Molly... I was just wondering when you will be here. Or if you're coming at all? Please call back. Uhm, bye." Molly's voice cracks multiple times from trying to keep all the pain in and stop the tears from pouring out of her.

*Is it my fault? Was I rude or did I talk too much?* She thinks. *He was supposed to be our savior.*

And just like that all of the dreams she'd dreamt up slowly fade. Instead of happiness, she is full of sorrow, she had just lost something she never even had. Yet it feels so painful, he could have been the voice she needed, the one to get her out of the traumatic life she's living.

She shakes her head and takes a deep breath. After all, it is her birthday, and she will not let anything ruin it.

"He isn't coming," she announces to her mother.

"I'm sorry sweetie. He's probably just drowning in self-pity, and feels bad for not being here sooner." Jen responds.

*What's self-pity?* Molly wonders. *If he feels bad for not being there before then why is he still not here? He said he was going to make up for it.*

She gives off a forceful smile to convince her mom that she's alright.

"Can we eat cake?" she asks, trying to distract herself.

"Yeah, let's eat tacos first," Jen replies.

Jen begins to dish out a meal for each kid. Molly getting the first meal as a birthday privilege.

"Thank you," Molly says.

As she starts eating her taco she hears the hotel door open and two people walk in.

"Hey, sweetie! Happy birthday!" her Father says as he comes walking in with her brother.

"Dad!!" she yells while throwing her plate to the side and running into his arms.

His name is Samuel but he goes by sam. As far as Molly is concerned, this is her father. She really has no idea what "biological" means, and she doesn't care to know. Dollan didn't show up to her birthday, which is a huge deal to Molly. But not Sam, he always shows up. No matter what. Molly has loved and adored Sam all of her life, she doesn't see that ever-changing.

"Here's your present." her brother says with a smile. They both have the same hair and eye color, reddish-brown hair, and hazel eyes, they could possibly pass for twins if he wasn't a few inches taller than her.

That's Samuel the 4th, but we call him Little Sam. He is 2 years older than Molly. On Molly's Father's side of the family, they have gone through generations of the name Samuel. Her Dad is the 3rd and her brother the 4th. Molly has adored her brother since birth, they do absolutely everything together. They play with toy cars, nerf guns, coloring in coloring books, and scooters for hours and hours. They even experience the excruciatingly painful scooter ankles together, they have attempted so many scooter tricks that have backfired, their ankles are now scarred. When they fail their tricks and that scooter comes swinging back around it hits their ankles and leaves literal mental pain. All together, Molly loves her brother more than just about anyone and she would do anything for him. Even if it means playing video games for hours and learning about toy cars together. As long as they do it together, Molly is all for it.

"Thank you!" Molly replies while giving him a great big hug.

"We can't stay for long but we'll stay for cake and presents!" Sam says.

"Ok." her smile widens. Her cheeks throb from smiling so big.

Molly and her brother run over to the table and begin to play with the toy cars' he'd brought.

"Which car do you want?" he asks. They're two cars, one blue and one red.

"Red," Molly replies. Red is her favorite color, plus her brother's favorite color is Blue.

They play for a long while. Driving their little cars up furniture and along the walls. Sometimes even ride through the air. Eventually, they get tired and want to do something else.

"Mom, can we eat the cake yet?" Molly asks

"Yeah, let me prepare the candles. Go sit on that chair. Everyone else gathers around the table." Jen says.

Jen begins putting candles on the cake, she puts 5 total. Representing Molly's age. She lights the candles and walks it towards the table.

"Happy birthday to you, happy . . ." everyone starts singing.

Molly feels herself exit the present event. She hears the singing in the background but the sound is muffled. Her thoughts start wondering as she thinks about what to wish for.

*All I want is for things to be different, for things to be like before. Before he came around, everything was fine before he came around. He has taken everything from me, from us. He took my most valuable thing.* Molly's thoughts wander. *He took my voice. . .*

"Make a wish!" her father says with a large smile.

What could she wish for? What could change things so drastically for Molly? If her voice isn't enough, then how could a wish be any different?

*I don't know what I want. Mom says it's all fine, and she makes it feel normal. I'm always scared, I just . . . I just want every day to be like this one.* Molly thinks for a wish. *I wish to be happy.* She blows out the candles in prayer.

Everyone cheers. And at that very moment, Molly feels something spark upon her veins. Everything begins to unmute itself and she feels a new sense of courage, it's nothing like she's ever felt before. Something is riding within herself, within her blood. But what? What could make her feel so alive and fearless?

All the sudden emotions' make Molly smile. A powerful smile that causes her cheeks to flare with warmth.

"What'd you wish for?" Amity asks.

"I can't tell you. If I tell you it won't come true," she says, still her smile present and vibrant.

Even though she feels these new magnificent emotions, she still feels the ones from before. All the pain, sorrow, and anger. But suddenly she feels strong enough to take it all on. Growth is upon her.

The kids begin shoving cake in their mouths . . . and somehow it ends up on both Molly and her brother's face. Molly starts the tease, but shortly it becomes a full-on war. The cake is being thrown all over the place by every kid. There is cake everywhere, it's even in places you know cake should not be in.

Jen discovers the fight that is going on just nearly feet away from her and stops the battle between the sugar-coated 5-year-olds, and 7 year old.

"Hey, stop it, the cake is supposed to be eaten not thrown. Go clean yourselves off, now please." her mother speaks over the yelling kids.

All of the kids begin to clean themselves off.

"I got more cake on your face," Amity whispers to Molly as she cleans off her face.

*~ Passion From Within ~*

Molly giggles as she wipes off all the thick sugary frosting. She finds frosting everywhere, though most of it is in her hair.

Finally, everyone is clean. Molly starts to open presents from her friends and family, she gets coloring books and other fun toys she can use in her next toy town game. It shortly ends and the kids split from the adults. The adults sit and chat. While all the kids continue to play and cause a ruckus throughout the hotel room. Molly runs around following every step her brother makes. Soon enough everyone gets tired and one by one the kids have sugar crashes. Molly is the first to fall along the bed and watch the cartoons playing on TV.

"We're going to head out, ok? I love you and happy birthday." her father says while kissing her on the forehead.

"Ok, I love you too," she replies, mid-yawn.

"Ready Lil Sam?" her father says as he nudges her brother who is almost asleep.

"Hm? Yeah, ready." Little Sam says as he manages to awaken himself. "By Molly, love you."

"I love you too," she replies softly, as she hugs his sleepy body.

Amity, Molly, and her Nana are the only ones left awake. Jen had left a little bit ago, but Molly doesn't know where. Liz and Camry are already asleep on the bottom bunk bed.

The hotel room is dark but the TV lights up some of the room. Molly and Amity are resting on the big bed closest to the main room door.

"Hey I want to show you something," Amity says with a little giggle. She grabs a glow light stick from out of the party supplies and a colorful book Molly had gotten for her birthday from Amity.

Amity goes under the bedsheet and Molly follows. Amity turns the glow stick on and it lights up with changing neon colors.

"Woah," she says while looking around. Letting her eyes follow the vibrant lights.

"Wait for the cool part," Amity replies. She opens the book and instant light glows from inside. The colors from within the book are being magnified by the light. It's beautiful. Molly's never seen anything like it. It's so colorful and vibrant. The colors are truly amazing. "Pretty cool right?"

"It's so pretty," Molly replies as she stares deep into the art.

She quickly becomes tired and releases a yawn. She lays down and closes her eyes.

"Can I sleep in this bed?" Amity asks.

"Yeah I'll go sleep on the top bunk," she says while trying to force her eyes open.

Molly crawls out from under the sheet and makes her way up the bunkbed ladder and into the bed. Her Nana turns the TV off. Molly closes her eyes and feels the room become darker. Right before she falls asleep, a question pops into her mind.

*Where's mom?* She wonders.

She suddenly feels a little burst of energy, the question makes her curious. Molly lays there wide-eyed waiting for her mom to walk through the door. She looks around trying to find a visible time somewhere. There isn't a single alarm clock except for the one near the bigger beds and those are tilted away from

~ *Passion From Within* ~

Molly. She feels herself become even more tired, her eyes begin to sting and ache. She fights it as hard as she can, she wants to wait so badly to see if her mom is alright. She fights on a few moments longer until she loses control and dozes off.

. . .

A sudden slam comes from the opposite side of the room. Molly slowly opens her eyes while feeling a sting from the bright light coming in from the hotel hallway. There are people leaving, it's hard to tell who.

"But mom . . ." Liz says.

"Sh, everyone is sleeping." Liz's Mom replies.

They exit the room with the door slamming behind them.

*Liz? Why is she leaving so early?* Molly wonders.

Her mother comes walking through the door with food in hand.

"Mom?" Molly says, rubbing her eyes and wondering if she is still dreaming.

"Goodmorning sweety." her mom replies.

"Why did Liz just leave?" she looks around the room and also realizes her grandmother is gone. "And where is Nana?"

"Oh, Liz's family had an event they needed to get to, and Nana had a meeting she needed to get to today."

*An event? It looked like Liz wanted to stay. Maybe she didn't, she never said anything about it. I must be overreacting again. . .* Molly thinks.

"Oh, ok," she says.

"Are you hungry? Would you like some food?" Jen asks.

"Sure." she gets up and crawls down the ladder. She walks over to the table and grabs the food her mother set out for her.

*Where was she last night?* She wonders. *It doesn't matter, she's here now.*

"Are those waffles?" Amity says as she pops up out of bed. Amity and Molly love waffles with powdered sugar on them, it's their thing.

"Yes, there are some here for you." Jen answers.

"Yes!" Amity whispers to herself. Amity sits down next to Molly and they scarf down their waffles." I bet I could eat mine the fastest." Amity says.

"No," Molly replies.

"Let's race at the count of 3."

"Ok" Molly prepares her fork in hand for the second Amity says three.

"1. . .2. . .3!" Amity shovels the waffle into her mouth as fast as she can.

Both the girls take bite after bite, each putting more in their mouths than they should. Amity starts to giggle as she looks over at Molly. Molly has powdered sugar all across her face, most of it is piled onto her cheeks. She giggles along with Amity. They giggle so hard that Amity gets powdered sugar up her nose and sprays it out.

Molly loses it, she is crying from all the laughter. Her cheeks and belly throb from the humor. Jen joins in with all the laughing once she realizes what has happened. Amity laughs so hard she almost chokes on the leftover waffle in her mouth.

Powdered sugar is everywhere. It's along the chairs, the table, and all of their food. Amity runs into the bathroom to clean off the powder all across her face and clothing.

Molly and her mother continue sitting at the table with tears spilling down their cheeks. Amity had sprayed the sugar like an elephant.

"Yeah yeah, I guess you won," Amity says as she walks back in.

"Yeah, I did!" Molly replies, trying to stop laughing so hard.

The girls continue to giggle as they clean up the mess. Camry soon awakens and gets out of the bottom bunk.

"Where's Liz?" Camry asks.

"She had to leave for a family event," Jen replies.

"Oh?"

Now that all the girls are awake they get their suits on and enjoy the hotel before they have to check out and head back to Jen's house. They spend around 3 hours playing in the huge waterpark and the colorful arcade. Once all the fun is over it comes time to check out and leave. Jen packed up the room while the girls were playing.

"You girls ready?" Jen asks.

"Yeah." Amity answers for everyone.

Molly doesn't want to leave. She doesn't want to go back to reality, she wants to keep this happiness forever. But sadly that isn't possible. Still, Molly refuses to answer, because saying it out loud will make her feel even worse.

The girls grab their bags and exit the room. Molly exits last, she looks upon the room and all of its objects. She tries to hold on to happiness and hold back the tears, but it's practically inevitable.

"C'mon Molly." her mother says as she walks down the hallway.

"Coming . . ." Molly replies.

Everything after that becomes a blur to Molly; checking out of the hotel, her friends leaving, even how she got home. Before she knows it she is sitting on the couch in their living room playing with Amity and some of the new toys she had gotten for her birthday.

"Look!" Amity says while holding up a drawing.

Molly feels herself flood back to the present. She feels reality settle in, her tummy aches at the realization.

"You're not looking," Amity says with a frown.

Molly looks up into the colorful art and smiles. It's beautiful, the way it swirls and fades into different shapes. The drawing may have many different shapes but they blend so perfectly.

"I love it," Molly replies giving off a genuine smile.

"Thank you," Amity says she expresses her satisfaction in Molly's comment.

Just as Molly goes to reply she hears a knock on the front door.

"Must be your mom," Molly says while turning her head back to the drawing.

"Molly, come here," Jen calls out.

Molly walks over to the front door, and there.

There he is.

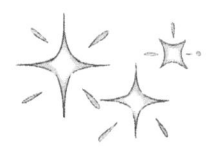

Chapter 7

# A Moment Within The Universe

Molly's heart drops.

It couldn't be.

Could it?

"Hey sweety." her Papa says while pulling Molly into a big bear hug.

"Papa!" she yells in joy.

Her heart fills with warmth. His presence gives her a breath of relief and comfort. She knows everything will be alright now that he is here.

"So Hunny, we have some news." her mother says while walking in from the front entryway.

She tilts her head in curiosity. *More surprises?*

"You're going to come to stay with us for a little while." her Papa says, smiling in an attempt to comfort Molly.

She vacillates from her Papa's big hazel eyes into her Mother's vibrant green eyes. Her mother looks troubled and in pain with the news. Molly feels her stomach drop as worries flood into her head.

"Is something wrong?" She asks.

"No. Nothing's wrong. You're just going to spend the summer with . . . with your grandparents." her mom says, trying to keep her emotions together. Her voice is full of pain and defeat.

Molly stares into her Mother's eyes, trying to understand what's going on and why. "Ok?" she replies.

"Here, I already packed your bag," Jen says while handing Molly a backpack and her elephant stuffie. The elephant stuffie Jen had given to Molly when she was in a treatment facility.

Molly looks between her Papa and Mother. *Leaving for a summer? Why would mom make a plan that makes her sad?* She wonders. *I can't leave her, what if something happens when I am gone and I can't protect her?*

"You guys better get going, I have to take Amity home." Jen says as she crouches down to Molly. "I love you so much, don't ever forget that. Ok?"

"Ok . . . I love you too." Molly says as she looks deep within her mother's eyes.

She grabs onto Molly's head and kisses along her forehead. Her mother's fear and sorrow are worn upon her ora.

Jen slowly backs away and releases Molly, for who knows how long.

Molly looks back with her eyes locked on her Mother. She has pulled away into a new reality, hand in hand with her Papa.

Along the long-lasting car ride, Molly dwells on many thoughts and worries. She wonders why she is leaving so suddenly. She wonders why her mom looked so hurt and scared. She does her best to not give in to the worries but it is impossible.

The sky is a depressing grey, no clouds in sight, not even a speck of blue within the sky. The grey clouds are so full of darkness it looks as if it'd soon be night. Shortly raindrops start hitting the truck's clear glass, each drop hitting faster each time. She feels her painful worries appear throughout her head. All kinds of worries about her mom.

She rests her head along with the window and feels the vibration of the car ride along her head. *How can I protect her this time? What if . . .*

"You are my sunshine, my only sunshine . . . you make me *happy* when skies are grey. You'll never know dear how much I love you . . . please don't take my sunshine away." her Papa sings along to the radio.

Molly looks over at her Papa and smiles. All of her worries fade as she feels his presence soothe her.

Throughout the rest of the car ride, Molly and her Papa create imaginative stories. Whenever they drive for a long period of time they make stories, taking turns back and forth as to what happens next in the story. The outcome can be quite eccentric at times, but their stories pass time quickly and before they know it they are driving up the dirt road leading to their driveway.

On the side of the dirt-road flowers sprout in the ditch and into the thick woods. The woods are full of oak and pine trees, thick of grass and nature. Molly loves to explore the woods surrounding her grandparent's home, it's so quiet and lone. She enjoys the silence of the woods, it makes her feel in control of her thoughts. Unlike being in her mother's house, there everything makes Molly feel overwhelmed, to the point of suffocation.

They pull up her grandparent's long steep driveway. At the top, a moderate-sized house sits with an attached garage at the left-hand side, and further down to the left a large two-door garage rests. The view of brown trim and widespread space gives Molly comfort. She is home.

Her Papa parks the car by the front entrance. As soon as the car stops Molly opens her door and hops out onto the damp woodchips. She inhales the scent of wet pine, closing her eyes and tilting her head upwards into the dark grey sky. She feels the breezy mist cover her face. She is comforted.

Running to the front door she feels the welcome matt lay beneath her feet. Grabbing onto the damp door handle she feels familiarity spark within her. Walking into the home she sniffles in the smell of freshly cooked food, feeling a rumble of eager hunger from her tummy, she walks on. Looking around, spotting the familiar furniture. She is relieved.

"Nana!" she yells out as she runs into her grandmother's arms.

"Molly! Hi sweety." her Nana says, griping onto Molly tightly. Slowly she pulls apart from Molly and looks into Molly's big hazel eyes.

Molly is consumed by her grandmother's stare, a feeling of safety flares within her. Everything fades away, nothing else matters anymore, she is protected from whatever may frighten her. Here. Here she is safe, it is her safe haven. The one place throughout the entire world, she feels anything is possible. Any happiness that appears here, feels infinite and everlasting.

"Are you hungry?" her Nana asks.

"Yes!" she replies with a huge smile.

Her Nana's name is Fidum. She is a medium-sized lady with short cut brown hair and light brown eyes. Molly adores her Nana, they do many things together, such as baking, arts and crafts, gardening, and play board games.

"Good, I made Taco hot dish and dinner rolls to go with it."

Molly's Papa comes walking in with her bags and walks them upstairs.

Her Papa goes by Solat. He is a tall man with short cut black hair and big hazel eyes. Molly is fascinated by his cooking or riding snowmobiles or four-wheelers, everything down to the way he walks. They do many things together, everything they do teaches Molly valuable life lessons, she absolutely loves it. He amazes her with everything that he does, she loves him beyond words.

"Let's go prepare the table." her Nana says.

~ Riley Brett ~

She follows her Nana into the big open kitchen and begins to feel all of the objects bring back memories. Nothing's changed, all of the pictures, pottery, and small nic nacs aligned just as they were before.

Together they prepare the table for dinner. Every meal they share together is sat upon the same chairs, nobody ever seeks change. Molly sits adjacent to her Papa and her Nana sits along her right side.

Molly takes the first seat as her Papa walks in from upstairs.

"Mmm, it smells great." her Papa says.

"Why thank you," Nana replies with a rosy-cheeked smile. "Go sit down I'll bring the food over."

"Let me help, you've been working hard." Papa insists.

"Ok, take these to the table. I'll get the rest. Thank you." Nana looks deep into papa's hazel eyes and gives off a genuine smile.

Papa rubs nana's shoulder in hopes to soothe her mind from the stress life brings her. Despite Nana's strength, life can take a toll on her too. It can all get a little much sometimes, but with loved ones by your side, anything is possible.

All three of them sit upon the table and pray. Pray in thanks for the food on the table, a roof over their heads, and in hopes, their loved ones will remain safe. They would pray in thanks to good health, but papa is sick. He has a lung illness that he has to fight every day. Despite the pain, it brings him he lives with kindness and selflessness. Even on his bad days, he finds a way to see the light and keep everything ever so positive. He sees the best in people even when they themselves cannot see it. The way he carries himself makes everyone aspire to be a better version of themselves. Molly especially, she aspires to be just like him someday. Everything he does, she wants to be exactly like him.

Everyone digs in after their prayers conclude.

"So, how was your drive up?" Nana asks.

"It was good. We told stories and sang along to the radio." Papa says with a contagious smile.

Molly giggles as she remembers the goofy stories they shared along the car ride. She giggles so hard she almost spills food from her mouth.

"Careful, you don't want to choke," Nana says with concern.

Molly calms herself and continues with her dinner.

The sky darkens as night rolls in. A sunset falls just west of the big brown home. Bugs buzz around the nightfall, swarming around the outside house lights.

Everyone finishes eating and clears their dishes. Nana and papa clean up the kitchen while Molly heads into the sunroom just off of the dining room. She sits down onto the footrest next to a resting instrument case. Curiosity crawls through her mind as she stares along the dark brown case.

"Papa, what's this?" she calls from the secluded room.

"Just a moment," Papa says as he finishes drying a dish from dinner.

She continues to study its odd shape, trying to figure out what it could be.

Papa walks into the room and looks over at the case. "Oh, that? That's a banjo." he says while picking up the case.

"What's a banjo?"

"Well, it's an instrument." he opens the case and glides his fingers along the wooden edge. "Follow me. I'll play it for you."

They walk into the kitchen and Molly hops up onto the countertop. She lets her eyes follow his fingers as he tunes the instrument. She watches as he picks along each string, a sound comes from off the instrument with each pluck. Nothing like Molly has ever heard, it's deep in one moment but high in another. She's intrigued.

Papa begins to play along the strings, he slowly builds into a structured song. With each echoed string giving off a loving contribution to her harmed body. Each string builds up what had been broken within her. Her mind sews itself stronger than before. Something she could have never imagined being possible. Her Papa gives to her rather than others who have taken. Taken everything she consists of, things she didn't even know she had. Noc took all of it. As if it was a thing, a product, an object. Something. Anything, that he could take whenever he pleased. Molly watched Noc strip her mother of everything she had. Everything. Down to the very last teardrop. They were his objects. Used but never gifted.

Molly feels herself live in the present tense. She lives within every key the banjo plays. Letting her body feel every tone of every melody. For once she feels full control of everything she has, from every limb upon her body to every emotional nerve.

She feels everything thrive from within her, every characteristic she aspires to have. It's there. Papa gives her that power, the power to persevere.

Papa lessens his play on all the strings and slowly comes to an end. Molly looks up into his big hazel eyes. And at that moment. The world disappears. It is only him and her. In one single moment of time. A moment the universe will soon leave but never forget. . .

"That's a banjo," Papa says.

*I could listen to him play the banjo forever.* She thinks, obsessing over the music.

"I love it," Molly responds.

"Me too," he says with a smile. "Let's go get ready for bed."

"Ok." she walks herself up the stairs with Papa in her tracks.

She runs into her grandparent's room and plops onto the couch." I love it here." she sprawls herself across the cushions and feels her skin against the rough fabric.

"Why's that?" Nana asks as she walks into the room.

"Well, I don't know. I just feel safe here."

"Safe?"

"Yeah, and comfortable. At home."

Nana looks at papa. They wonder upon Molly's words. Mainly why Molly is using such big words at such a young age, and why those words specifically. Safe and Comfortable? Why those words, shouldn't she always feel *safe*?

Molly gets herself ready for bed. Including the sloppy cleaning of teeth in the bathroom. She tends to dance while brushing her teeth. The smell of fresh mint stays on her body for the rest of the night due to the springing of toothpaste all over the place. She always brushes her teeth alongside her grandparents, it's a nightly routine of theirs. From there they will make their way into the big bed and enjoy a storytime.

"What story tonight?" Papa asks.

"You pick," Molly says.

Papa picks out a book and begins to read the fictional tale. Molly feels herself getting sleepier by the minute. Hearing her papa read a story soothes her mind tremendously. Everything he says and the way he says it, his words assure her that everything will be ok. Word by word, her eyes get heavier until she can't hold up the weight.

*Tense air fills the room.* Molly's body tosses and turns. *Blank grey walls close her in. Halls and halls fill the house. Footsteps creek from above. Molly runs down the hall as fast as she can, but no matter how fast she runs the steps get closer. She turns around and runs the opposite way but it's useless. The sound of each footstep on the floorboards above her crawl up along her spine. Molly looks over and sees a window seat below a wall, but no window. The only windows are above her eye level. No escape, just the matter of embracement. She feels her fear scratch upon her strength. Tearing away at what had just been built. The steps get closer, louder, and heavier. Until they are directly above her. Unable to move she lays there and realizes the stuffed animals from back in her mother's house are along her lap. It isn't real, she is dreaming. But still, she cannot escape the inner nightmare. The nightmare that haunts her of her demons. Creeks and cracks sound from throughout the house. The dark, somber house. Nothing but soaked must and fear fill the air. But not just from herself. She feels another presence, someone else is here. Close. Close enough to give her a chill that stabs from inside her. It isn't real. . . it isn't real . . .it isn't real. . . she whispers into the night.*

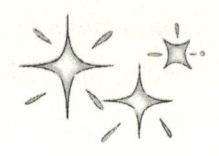

## Chapter 8

# A Saving Breeze

Molly wakes to birds chirping from outside. As the birds sing their early morning songs, she feels stress lift from her body. The songs from each bird give joy to Molly's ears. Despite the happy awakening, a chill rides up her arms as she remembers last night's nightmare. So vividly. So real. How was it just a dream? How was she so confined to such an intense nightmare?

She shakes it off and remembers where she is. She's home. Looking over she sees the spot where her grandparents had laid asleep. She sits herself up and takes in the smell of freshly baked pancakes. A smile fills her face as she remembers the taste of her grandfather's magnificent pancakes. Those pancakes can solve any problem, no matter how problematic. Thinking of it makes her tummy rumble.

~ *Passion From Within* ~

Her body is overly filled with excitement. Every single part of her body feels relaxed and cared for. She feels protected. Something that is so very uncommon for Molly, it almost feels weird. She can't help but think about her mother and have a concern about her safety. But there is *nothing* she can do about it. After all, she is only 5. She has so many thoughts that are confined to her tiny innocent body, with no way to release them. Because she is too scared to speak out about how she truly feels, and what really goes on behind the walls of the baby blue-trimmed house. Finding her inner voice isn't the difficult part, it is knowing how to express it and use it. It is hard for her to admit she doesn't know how, but she can find it from within herself to trust the process. Even if it means having nightmares *every* single night. She perseveres through all of it, simply by trusting that "everything will be ok".

Molly runs down the stairs, each foot causing an echo throughout the home. Her little feet are bare and ready for adventure. She continues her run into the kitchen where both her grandmother and grandfather sit amongst themselves with their steamy morning coffee. The steam rises into swirls within the air, shortly vanishing into the early morning hours.

"Goodmorning sweetheart," Nana says.

"How'd you sleep?" Papa adds.

"Good Morning. Good . . ." Molly replies.

She walks over and sits down in her usual spot.

They spend their morning eating breakfast and planning the day ahead. But she doesn't know what's to come, her grandparents had said it is a surprise. All she can think about is how horrible she is with surprises. She can only hope it isn't as badly ending as the last.

"Go pack an overnight bag. We will prepare the rest." Nana says.

Everyone goes off on their separate ways to complete their individual tasks. Molly only dwells on the worries instead of what good could come. She can't help it, the constant alert for everything. It is hard to break that kind of habit once it has already been formed.

They gather back together and stack their items by the door.

"Ready?" Papa asks.

*I hope it is a good surprise.* She thinks.

"Yep," Nana says as she walks behind Molly out of their home.

As Papa stacks their bags into the car Molly hops in the car and gets herself situated, hoping that she will be prepared for whatever happens.

Her mind wanders off as they pull out of their driveway. She thinks about the nightmare from last night and how she couldn't escape it. She knew she was dreaming yet she couldn't move nor escape the dream itself. It was as if she entered a whole different reality and she couldn't get out of it unless someone had woken her.

Aside from all the pain and troubles, she looks deep into the sky and lets the clouds consume her. The imagination involved truly takes her in for everything she is and can be. Imagining amongst the sky inspires her, it shows her that dreams aren't all evil. That is the one and the only thing she trusts, completely. She lets herself be vulnerable to all the possibilities her dreams can bring. Her guard is always on high alert, but not for this. For this, she gives her all and that inner spark. Inner passion. It could ignite a flame she never saw coming. One that can inspire her to find *her* deeply buried voice.

Shortly the car ride comes to an end as they pull into a parking lot.

"We're here!" Papa says.

"Isn't this the parking lot that leads back to the cabin?" Molly asks.

"Yes, it is," Nana replies with a smile.

"Yay!" Molly feels her body boil with excitement.

"Alright now, grab your bag Molly and let's get unpacked," Papa says.

Molly hops out of the car and sees dirt fly up from under her feet. The cool midday breeze picks up the loose dirt and carries it away to who knows where. She feels adventure spark from inside, her patience is weakening. She can not wait to explore throughout the cabin and the woods surrounding.

"Let's go, let's go!" she says while jumping up and down with eager desire.

"Hold on sweety we have to get our things," Nana replies to Molly's eagerness with a giggle.

"Here carry this," Papa says as he hands Molly a cooler.

She takes the cooler and feels the weight pull down on her arm.

"Is it too heavy?" He asks.

"No, I got it," Molly says, puffing out her chest trying to sound tough.

"Alright, does everyone have everything?" Nana asks.

"Yep," Papa replies.

Molly is still struggling with the weight of the cooler. She tries her very best to not show how hard she is struggling. But every minute that goes by, her arm feels as they'll give out any second to come.

They are walking deep down the trail, over big rocks, roots that have made their way across the trail, and puddles of water to the sides. Everyone wheres exhaustion, with each step they slow their pace.

"Maybe we should take a quick break," Nana says.

Everyone plops down onto something, Molly sits on the cooler, Papa sits on a rock, and Nana sits on a patch of dirt. They take their time with the rest and recharge their energy.

Nana looks a little antsy to get back on the walk. Or itchy, Molly can't tell.

"Wow, I must have gotten bitten by mosquitos last night," Nana says as she itches her legs.

"What do you have ants in your pants?" Papa asks.

"Very funny," Nana replies with a roll in her eyes and a giggle.

"Uhm, Nana. There are some ants crawling on you." Molly replies.

There is a whole swarm of them, all over Nana.

"Oh shoot there are ants in my pants!" Nana yells. She jumps up and tries to shake them all off, she runs along the trail in hopes they will get out of her clothes. She is in a panic, they are biting with a tickle and an itch.

"Are you ok?" Molly asks, trying not to laugh at her grandmother's funny dance.

"Get them off!" Nana giggles at her simple mistake. Still running around in hope to escape the ants and their deceitful crawl.

"Maybe we should run to the cabin so you can change out of the ant pants," Papa says, trying to contain his laugh.

"Yes, let's do that!" Nana makes her way down the trail. "C'mon Molly."

Molly makes her way behind them, not knowing what to do besides carry the heavy cooler.

Nana runs down the trail as quickly as she can and makes her way far ahead of Molly and her grandfather. Papa can't run due to his illness, his lungs are too fragile to be put under that kind of intense activity.

Shortly Molly can't see her grandmother anymore. Molly makes her way to the cabin, side by side with her grandfather.

"Are you excited?" Papa asks.

"Yes! I can't wait." Molly says. "I hope Nana can escape the ants though." she no longer holds back her laugh.

Papa laughs along with her." We should probably help her." he replies.

"Yeah," Molly says.

They make their way to the cabin driveway, Papa walks in front of Molly and makes his way up to the cabin.

"Are you coming?" Papa asks.

"Yeah I'll be right there," she replies.

She stops in the midst of her walk and takes in the view of the beautiful log cabin. The stunning view of the lake through the thin woods. A warm breeze brushes along her face, she breathes in the fresh air and feels it sink deep into her lungs. All of the toxic air from before is no longer there, it is pushed into the past. Only a memory to be brought upon her mind when she feels like it. A smell of creek water fills the breeze. She holds this moment, for as long as she possibly can. For everything that it is and all that it has to offer. Her eyes close as she takes it all in, it is just her and the saving warm breeze.

The cabin door slams behind Papa and snaps Molly back into the present. She runs to the cabin door and sets the cooler to the side of it. A rush of familiarity and comfort hits her, she feels so much comfort fill all throughout her body. She opens the door and walks upon the hardwood floor. Everything is as it was before, down to the hanging stovetop popcorn.

"Oh my goodness, that feels better," Nana says, walking in with a new pair of pants.

Molly giggles.

"Are you laughing at me?"

"No . . ." Molly says sarcastically.

Everyone laughs at Nana's funny incident.

*~ Passion From Within ~*

Once the laughter fades they begin to put away their items. Sweat drips from Molly's forehead as she carries the cooler in. "It's really hot in here." she says.

"Yes, it is. You could go swimming Molly, we'll come to sit on the dock and watch you." Nana replies.

"Ok!" she's relieved that there is a way to cool down from the torturous heat.

She gets her swimsuit on and waits impatiently by the cabin door for her grandparents to follow her. The sweat drips down every inch of her body, she feels as if she's being baked alive. Her skin is burning at the idea of ice-cold water-consuming her skin. The thought of her head going under it and cooling her hot thick hair makes her more anxious.

"Ok. Are you ready Molly?" Papa asks.

"Yes!" Molly says dreadfully baking upon the hot air.

She steps out of the cabin, running along the hot ground. Feeling as if hot coals are beneath her tiny feet. She watches the lake get closer with every footstep taken. The tree branches beside her blow in the hot breeze, filling the air with a pine fragrance. She runs along the narrow trail leading to the dock floating upon the water. Her footsteps reach the planks making up the dock, her hair flying within the sweet cool breeze from off the lake. Everybody part feeling the coolness and freedom of the beautiful lake. She runs along every plank until she reaches the last and springs her leg, leaping into the water. The lake buries her with its dense water and ripples from her entrance. She lays deep beneath the water, letting it take her in and keep her within its peaceful silence. Every part of her is consumed by the chilled water, its silence brings her comfort. She's able to feel things she couldn't before. Each water molecule making its way through every strand of hair, cooling down her burning head. She watches each bubble of oxygen leave her body as she stays down deep upon the water. Each bubble narrowing the longer she stays. As every bubble leaves her lungs she swims to the surface and takes a deep breath, feeling it cover her lungs in the protection of the saving breeze.

Molly learned to swim from her grandfather a year ago. She has always been scared to fully enter the water, head under, and everything. But with this hot summer day, that fear no longer matters.

She spends the rest of the afternoon swimming in the water and enjoying the scenery. Her grandparents gather their fishing supplies and fish off the dock. Now and then Molly joins in and tries to catch a fish. Her grandfather teaches her to fish and how to cast the fishing line far into the lake. He says "the key to fishing is patience". She listens to all of his advice as they sit along the dock, feet hanging off into the water. The best part of fishing is getting to spend time with the people surrounding you. For Molly and her grandparents, this is always true, they spend most of their time talking and laughing until their cheeks grow soar.

As the sky darkens stars begin to appear. They lay along the dock's surface and gaze into the shining constellations, trying to create stories out of the wondrous shapes. The moon reflects upon the shimmery lake, creating a night light for those who lay awake.

"Hey, look at that one. It looks like a pot." Molly says in fascination.

"That is called the Big Dipper, it is created by seven bright stars. You can always find it up north." Papa replies.

"Do you see that super bright star, right over there?" Nana asks. She points to a shining bright speck in the sky and says "That is the North Star. If you are able to find the Big Dipper, then you can find the North Star."

"Wow," Molly whispers.

The constellations amaze Molly, the way that they shine so bright upon the dark mystical sky.

A sound of crickets chirping and frogs croaking surround them. The warm breeze has turned into steady cool air. In the distance a loon's call echoes throughout the lake, hoping to find its family. Just as the call comes to an end, the entire lake turns quiet. Everyone looks up into the sky, in an effort to study the stars.

"Look there. It's a shooting star!" Molly says as she spots a rocketing light.

"Everyone make a wish," Papa replies.

The three of them close their eyes and wish upon their dreams.

*I wish I could hold on to this moment forever* . . . Molly makes her wish in the silence of her mind.

Before they know it the star vanishes and the night sky is back to shining constellations. Molly feels her hope rise as she gets comfortable with her new normal. The surprise didn't end badly, and that brings her the highest of hopes. She knows as long as she is with her grandparents she will be alright, and that is all that matters.

The mosquitos have bitten almost every inch of Molly's skin, the itch is getting violent. Bugs by the lake are always so much worse, especially at their cabin.

"Let's head back to the cabin, the bugs are getting worse," Nana says.

"Good idea. Come on Molly." Papa replies.

Molly brings herself to her feet. She is starting to feel all of the bug bites, they are everywhere. Places they should not be in. She fights herself, trying not to itch. But each second that goes by feels like hours. Step after step the pain makes its way to every bite throbbing and pulsing. They make it to the cabin steps, but Molly can't take it. She itches along the bites, instead of relieving her itch it puts her in pain.

"Don't itch. I will get the itch cream." Nana says, running into the bedroom.

She stands there still as can be, hoping if she doesn't move maybe it won't itch so bad.

"Here," Nana says, handing Molly the cream.

Molly bursts it open and slathers it onto her hands. She coats her body in layers on top of layers, trying to wane the painful itch.

"Thank you." Molly manages to say, still covering her skin in the relieving cream.

Still her body itches, but the temptation has gone down and so has the pain.

"Better?" Nana asks.

"A lot better."

"Good, I'm glad."

Molly is covered in the pink cream, she practically bathed in it.

"How about we get ready for bed, then we can read a bedtime story and eat popcorn?" Papa suggests.

"Yes!" Molly replies in a thrill.

"Alright, run along and get your PJs on," Nana says.

She runs into the bedroom and quickly prepares herself for bed. As she gets ready she hears pops begin upon the stovetop. The air soon fills with the smell of butter layered popcorn. Molly breathes it in and expedites her routine.

"Popcorn is done," Nana yells out.

Molly runs into the main room and inhales the smell of freshly made popcorn.

"Sit and snuggle in," Papa says.

They gather on top of the couch and cuddle in close.

"We are going to make our own story tonight," Nana adds in.

"Can I start?" Molly asks.

"Of course. Make it good." Papa says with a giggle.

"Once upon a time . . . there was a girl that ran through the woods and caught butterflies. She carried a basket with her wherever she went." Molly begins the story.

"She caught many butterflies, but one day she stumbled upon a house," Nana adds.

"And in that house, there was a kind witch. The witch spotted the little girl adventuring along the trail and decided to talk to her." Papa continues.

"The witch said hello and invited her inside her house. The little girl said no because she is a stranger, the little girl went walking on the trail again until . . ." Molly adds to the story.

"She ran into another little boy and offered him help with the apple he was trying to retrieve. The boy said no because she was a stranger. So the girl continued on along the trail until she saw a steep hill, she ran toward the hill when . . ." Nana continues.

"A great big wolf stopped her in her tracks and asked her for some food. The girl said no because he was a stranger. She began to run up the hill and eventually made it to the top, where she was greeted by a . . ." Papa creates more fiction.

"Old man, who told her she had a nice smile. The girl screamed and fell down the hill. Her basket dropped by the man and food spilled out . . ." Molly adds.

"Her lunch spilled everywhere, the cookies, sandwiches, and the fruit. The girl rolled all the way to the bottom and lay there in sadness because her food was gone. The starving man gathered her food and put it back into the basket. He slowly made his way down the hill and brought the girl her basket. Even though she screamed in his face and he was hungry for any crumb to spare, he gave her the basket full of food." Nana said.

"She took the basket and asked him why he brought it back to her even though she screamed in his face. He smiled and said "I'd rather you have it than me.", the girl picked out of her basket and gave him her sandwich. She smiled back and said "I am sorry for judging you so quickly." and she continued on her journey." Papa added.

Molly thinks deep into the stories meaning. She questions what it could mean. What lesson were her grandparents trying to teach her?

Suddenly a thought flares in her head. *Kindness.* Everyone deserves kindness, no matter how they look, whether they are a stranger or not, or even if they aren't very kind themselves.

"She ran on the trail and saw the boy again. She stopped and smiled at him, "I'd rather you have it than me." she said while handing him her cookies from in the basket." Molly smiled at the underlying meaning.

"The boy smiled, and she continued on. She walked along the trail until she reached the witch's house, where she knocked on the door. The witch opened the door, and the girl said "I'd rather you have it than me." she handed the witch her fruit from in the basket. From there she traveled home, with no food. But a day to remember." Nana finishes the story.

Molly snuggles in closer with her grandparents, so close she can hear their hearts beat. A yawn escapes her as she gets sleepy. She grabs ahold of her blanket trying to keep in as much heat as possible. She watches the clock tick from one second to the next until she is too tired to keep her eyes open.

~ Riley Brett ~

Her thoughts wander as she lays along with the cozy couch. *I wonder where mom is right now. I can't keep her safe from here, I hope she's ok . . .*

Molly's worries continue for hours until finally, she manages to fall asleep.

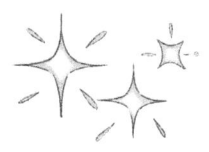

# Chapter 9
# The Beauty Of Patience

Sunshine fills the cabin, peeking through every reachable spot. The sound of dishes clinking comes from the kitchen. Molly forces her eyelids open, her nightmares had followed her into last night's rest. She stretches her soar body and lets out a yawn.

"Good Morning sleepyhead." Nana says, walking over to Molly. "Papa made breakfast, we didn't know when you'd wake."

Molly gets up off the couch and makes her way towards the appetizing smell. She steps closer trying to get a look, but can't tell what it may be. Instead, she takes a seat at the table and waits eagerly. The smell makes her mouth water. She can only imagine how delightful it will taste when she finally gets to eat it.

"Here you go." Papa sets a plate in front of Molly.

*~ Riley Brett ~*

There it is. A plate of freshly stacked pancakes covered in freshly picked berries and topped with homemade maple syrup dripping down the thick sides. To the side a freshly cut grapefruit prepared in perfectly cut wedges, just waiting to be eaten. She goes to take the beautiful first bite, covered in syrup.

"Hold on, wait for the rest of us to take a seat," Papa asks.

Molly feels her tummy rumble at the thought of waiting. She powers through the bubbling rumble. Guilt fills her cheeks, she feels bad for not waiting in the first place. They made this beautiful meal, and she didn't want to wait.

Moments go by until everyone is ready. Molly feels the anticipation fill her body.

*Just a few more seconds.* Molly tries to convince herself.

"You may eat now," Papa says.

Molly digs in. Her mouth floods with flavor; Sweet, sour, salty, and even savory. She feels the berries pop in her mouth with each chew, a blueberry burst, and crowds her taste buds. Every flavor works together creating a magnificent bite. Just one bite, the rest go by quickly as she shovels more into her mouth.

"Is it any good?" Papa asks.

Molly tries to swallow her food so she can reply.

"Silence is the best compliment." Nana smiles at Molly.

She shakes her head to agree, her mouth still stuffed. Laughs break loose between all around the table.

"It is really good," Molly says, as she manages to swallow the rest of her food.

"Good. We got the berries from a local berry farm and the syrup is from great uncle Henry." Papa replies.

"Yeah, my brother makes amazing maple syrup." Nana agrees.

Molly loses focus as she stares out of the window beside her seat. All of the tall grass blows in the wind, she can only imagine the cool breeze gliding along her face. Just like yesterday. Or the smell of pine trees filling the air. She can remember the smell so perfectly. The way the heat burned her body, and the relief she had felt once the water swallowed her whole. That feeling still rides along her skin.

"We're planning on heading home shortly. We will pack our things and start our walk back to the parking lot around 11." Papa says while he rinses his dishes in the sink.

Papa's comment snaps Molly back into the present.

"Once you are done eating please rinse your dishes and pack your bag," Nana adds.

"Ok," Molly replies. She feels her energy refill throughout her body.

She walks over to the sink and rinses her dishes. A little dance makes its way out of her while her happiness rises.

The sound of birds chirping fills the cabin walls and brings a smile to Molly's face. All of her surroundings bring such a variety of emotions, making her feel ever so happy.

Feeling the comfort ride along her skin and sink deep into her bones. Safety ringing within the air and guaranteeing the pain to stay away from here. Love glowing deep within her heart, consisting of care so dear she cannot fear. This feeling is everything she could ever wish to keep. If only she could stay upon this moment forever, eliminating the weeps.

The morning continues with packing and cleaning up. Until 11 o'clock approaches and they exit the cabin, heading to the spot they had left their car sitting. Molly takes her last look at the cabin and feels her eyes swell with tears. Not a single part of her wants to say goodbye, the cabin gives off a joy that is irreplaceable. Though she doesn't know why it hurts so much, going home to her grandparent's house should be no different. It is her home, but so is the cabin. The cabin is her home away from home.

"Bye for now," Molly whispers to the log cabin.

She runs along the trail, catching up to her grandparents.

"Hey, everything alright?" Nana asks while setting her hand on Molly's shoulder.

"Yep," Molly replies, following them down the trail and down to the car.

The sky is blue, but no clouds to be seen. Molly helps load the car in hopes to expedite the process.

"What do you say we catch butterflies when we get home?" Papa asks Molly.

"Yeah!" Molly replies with excitement.

She hurries into the car and settles herself onto the hot car seat. The air feels humid and dreadful. Nana turns the AC on and tilts the vent towards Molly. She feels the cold airbrush along her hot and sweaty skin, filling her with relief.

They pull out of their parking spot and drive along the highway. Molly stares out the window and watches waves roll along the water. Seagulls fly within the breeze, searching for fish beneath the water. She squints her eyes in an attempt to spot the shoreline across the big blue lake. She fails to see any sign of land, the only thing she has visibility of is the water spreading for miles. But even that disappears along the horizon.

The radio plays old songs, cutting in and out as they drive through poor service. Molly sings along when she can, she knows the songs well. She listens to all sorts of music when she is with her Papa, they love to sing and dance all around the kitchen. Just after dinner near every night, they turn on the radio and tune in a good station. Papa takes her by the hand and twirls her until she becomes dizzy. Then he pulls her in and she hops onto his feet. He leads them through the kitchen, one step at a time. They try their best to stay in beat with the songs, but some are just too fast. It never seems to stop them from trying their absolute best, they fight on trying to feel the rhythm of the song. Within those moments, Molly feels the happiness thrive from inside her. Those are the moments she can truly feel her voice, from there she doesn't know where to go. And like all moments, it comes to an end. Similar to the moment, her voice fades. She has no clue as to how to grip onto that voice, let alone how to hold on for dear life.

As the stations switch between genres, she hears many that remind her of those impactful moments.

~ *Riley Brett* ~

A sudden jolt travels through the car. Bringing Molly out of the beloved memory from the past. A deer caused the abrupt stop; which is very common in Votum. They continue along the road for many more miles, luckily no more deer slowing them down.

Molly is eager to get home and catch butterflies on the "Secret Trail". The trail leads through the woods alongside their home. It is called a secret for a reason.

They finally make it home, after all of her daydreaming and fiddling of thumbs.

Excitement prickles along her skin. "I am going to catch butterflies!" Molly says.

"Ok, be careful running through the woods," Nana replies.

"I'll be over shortly," Papa adds.

She hops out of the car the first chance she gets and runs along into the garage. There it is. A tall standing butterfly catcher, a pink mesh net is knit along the top. It hasn't always looked so pretty, there have been points in time where holes took up most of the net. Catching butterflies can be quite competitive. Not with others, only with herself. She loves to beat previous numbers, it brings her a new kind of thrill. Knowing she did better than last time gives her reassurance of all her *hard* work. She spends hours on top of hours catching butterflies. Most of the time it is because she won't let herself eat dinner until she beat her daily goal. She might be a little too hard on herself, but it brings her happiness and that can be rare to find.

She runs out of the garage, net in hand. Her feet crunch along the gravel driveway. The sky is bright blue and now full of large fluffy clouds. Happiness fills her cheeks and creates a glow. Alongside the big brown house, a trail spreads into the woods. She stops in front of the entrance, feeling all of the wondrous memories flood back. Breathing in she feels nature's fresh air fill her lungs, a smile spreads between her glowing cheeks. The sun hits her face as she tilts her head up into the sky, feeling every ray of sunshine heat her face. Her big hazel eyes look deep upon the traveling trail, seeing infinite opportunity. Sparking a flare within her mind, she acts upon the determination and runs. She runs as fast as she can, stepping over thick roots spreading across the widening path. Dirt flies up from the flick of her shoes, hitting the back of her legs. Wind crawls between each individual strand of hair, making her feel ever so free. Trees spread all along the trail's sides, hiding the trail from everyone. Their branches bounce in the wind, giving off a sweet pine scent. Peaceful silence surrounds the trail with all of its beauty. Molly makes her way to the end and stands. Silently taking in every last thing the trail has to offer. Her entire body in tune with itself.

Sun rays peeking through the leaves upon the tall trees. Lighting up the green grass, and magnifying the colors along the graceful butterflies.

Molly grips onto the handle.

*I need to catch 12 before I go inside.* She creates her daily goal.

She begins her journey and hops around the grassy ground. Three butterflies hover over her, one beautiful flap at a time.

She does her best to keep up with their quick movements. One lands on a bright yellow flower, Molly gets in her position to trap it as it flies away. She quickly swings her net over the moving butterfly, the net flies too slow and she misses. It makes its way over the tall trees.

"You'll get 'em next time," Papa says, walking in from the trail.

Molly giggles, "They're too fast."

"That doesn't mean you can't catch them. You don't have to be faster, you just have to be smarter."

"How do I get smarter?"

"Well, they fly the same. Wait until they land on a plant, then lay the net on top. Carefully, you don't want to hurt them."

Molly thinks deeply about the advice he gave her. *Smarter? Not faster.*

She searches for more butterflies. Her eyes scan the woods, along the tree edges, and along the flowers. No luck is found.

"Be patient, they will come," Papa says.

Molly thinks about that for a moment. She wonders why everything takes so much patience, and how being patient changes the number of butterflies coming. How can time and patience be the answer to so many things? What makes time so special?

"Ok, I will try," Molly responds.

She sits on the tree stump next to her grandfather.

"When you are patient you are able to enjoy the happiness in the present. Happiness can fly by within a matter of seconds if you take it for granted. Just like catching butterflies, if you forget to enjoy it you'll wonder where the day went."

Molly thinks more about his advice. *Patients? How can time go by so quickly but other times it goes by slowly? Enjoy the moment.* She takes a deep breath, trying to understand what his advice means.

She makes a hop and a skip over to her butterfly net, trying to feel the peacefulness of the woods again.

There it is. A beautiful flying butterfly, with orange and yellow markings all along its gorgeous wings. The butterfly is behind the trees making its way north.

*I have to catch that. I have never seen such a pretty butterfly.* Molly fascinates over its beauteous wings.

She runs towards it without hesitation. Soon enough her run turns into a sprint, she weaves her way between the branches and hurtles over the logs along the dirty ground. The butterfly flies away each time Molly gets closer. She forgets her grandfather's advice and tries to quicken her speed. The branches tear along her skin creating tiny scratches all along her body. Her legs burn at the intense speed she is pushing herself through. The butterfly begins to fly higher, Molly leaps in an attempt to capture it. . .

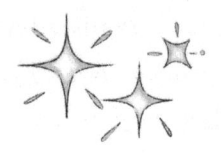

## Chapter 10

# A Shattering Heart

A blur overrides Molly's mind, the summer flashes by within moments. Fishing trips across small freshwater lakes. Camping on the secret trail. Bonfires down at the fire pit late at night, and making s' mores until the fire reaches its last flame. Stargazing until their eyes begin to burn from exhaustion. And most importantly, butterfly catching. Even though she didn't catch that one butterfly, she made it her summer mission to catch all the butterflies that came into her site.

She opens her eyes to a slightly lit up room. The sky is grey and dark, a huge thunderstorm is coming their way.

Rain clashes along the windows and sends a chill up her skin. The sky's gloom fills the room with a dim light. She keeps her body buried under the thick bedding, away from the cool dense air. Luckily today she doesn't have to go to school because it is a Saturday.

Molly started kindergarten two months ago, at a small school tucked away in a tiny town. It is a brick elementary school with very few kids. She doesn't like it very much, not the school itself but the kids. Bus rides to and from school are torturous for her. She is constantly being bullied, by the same kids every single day. The kids in the back of the bus bully her the most, they are two grades ahead of her. They tell her to go harm herself, sometimes they even threaten to hurt her themselves. She tries so hard to not listen. Most of the time it doesn't matter how hard she fights, the pain gets through and it breaks her heart. Piece by piece. Being constantly told how much of a failure she is making her think very low of herself and makes her feel the disappointment everyone must-have.

For two months she hid the pain, she didn't want anyone thinking she was weak. Especially her grandfather, she didn't want to let him down. So she wiped the tears away and pushed the sadness aside. Until her tears couldn't dry anymore, she got up the courage to tell her grandfather about the threats and mental abuse. He was so furious, the next day he had come with Molly to the bus. He talked to the boys and the bus driver. From that day on, they apologized and didn't say one more harmful word.

She did get a savior after all.

Lightning lights up the bedroom, and thunder shortly crackles throughout the sky. Molly sits down by the window and watches the rainfall upon the earth's surface. The water bounces as it collides along objects. She inhales the strong smell of a rainy day. Water droplets clash against the roof, making a sound that echoes through the home. Her skin prickles and her gut wrenches with fear. The feeling seems so familiar. Molly shakes the morning worries away and makes her way down the stairs.

A smell of freshly made coffee sits within the air. Voices whisper from in the kitchen. Molly approaches the bright room and sits at the table.

"Goodmorning," Nana says.

"How did you sleep?" Papa asks.

"Goodmorning, good," Molly replies in confusion. How did the summer fly by so incredibly fast?

"I am glad you are awake. I just got a call from the social worker and she will be stopping by around lunchtime. She has a few things she would like to go over with all of us." Nana says.

"About what?" Molly wonders.

"She didn't say. I'm sure it's nothing to worry about."

"Ok."

Molly yawns, trying to escape the early morning sleepiness.

Another strike of lightning lights up the sky, a crackle follows close behind.

"Wow, it's raining cats and dogs out there," Papa says, sipping from his steaming coffee.

An idea pops into Molly's head. "We should make thunder cake for the girl coming over."

"That's a great idea. I will help." Papa replies in kindness. "I will gather the materials."

Molly walks over to a drawer next to the sink and pulls out a cooking apron. She puts on the red and white apron and finds her stepping stool. They gather materials from around the kitchen and pile them onto the countertop.

"Oh wait, we need the book. We can't make thunder cake without the book." Papa reminds them.

"I will go get it." Molly volunteers.

She sets her stool down and runs to the staircase. Running up the stairs, a creek comes from every other step. A soft carpet spreads beneath her feet as she walks upon the third floor. From in the guest room, she grabs the book and stares at the cover.

*Thunder cake.* Molly reads in her head.

Thunder Cake is a book Molly's nana read to her often. Especially during thunderstorms. Molly loves the rain, but the thunder and lightning that come with it are not her favorite. On the other hand, her Nana loves the thunder and lightning. Molly doesn't understand why, but she wishes to.

Molly grips along the book's spine and runs down the stairs. She walks along into the kitchen and sees all of the ingredients laid out. They are ready for Molly to put it together and mix away.

"Can you open it up to the recipe page, please?" Papa says.

"What is a recipe?" Molly asks.

"A recipe explains step by step how to cook or bake something."

"Oh." Molly flips to the back of the book, where her grandmother and her would always read when done with the rest of the story.

*Thunder cake recipe.* Molly reads.

She sets the book down along the counter. Papa gathers the measuring materials.

"I will measure the ingredients, you can stir," Papa says.

"Ok," Molly replies, grabbing a mixing spoon.

Papa pours flour, sugar, and other dry ingredients into a big clear bowl. Molly watches carefully as the powdered items slide into the glass bowl.

"Can you grab a fork? It will work better to mix these dry ingredients." Papa asks.

"Yep," Molly replies, heading over to the silverware drawer. There she grabs a perfectly clean fork. "Can I mix them yet?"

"Hold on, let me add one more thing." Papa pours in the final dry ingredient. "Ok, now it is ready to be mixed."

Molly begins to mix the ingredients in the clear bowl. She shifts the individual items around until they are combined into one. "Finished."

"Ok, no we add the wet ingredients. Such as eggs." Papa continues to add more ingredients to the bowl until there are none left to add. "Ok, now we need to use the mixer."

Molly grabs the mixer from off the other counter. "Here you go."

"I'll tell you what. You can help me use the mixer, on low." Papa replies, putting the beats onto the mixer.

"Ok!" Molly has never been allowed to help with the mixer, she has always been told she was too young. Not anymore.

A smile fills her cheeks.

Papa puts his hands onto the mixer and Molly puts her hands on top. They turn the mixer on and glide it slowly along with the ingredients. Powder flies up the edges.

Molly's hand slips and a little powder fly into their faces. They quickly turn the mixer off and begin to laugh.

Flour is spread across the counter, along with their faces.

Papa wipes Molly's face-off, "Maybe we should go a little slower next time." he giggles.

"Next time? You mean I can help with the mixer again?" Molly says surprised.

"Of course, you are five now. You can help with those kinds of things."

Molly is beyond happy. Nobody has ever said she was old enough for anything besides making her own food. Her Papa has given her that power, to feel valid. Even though it is a small thing, to Molly it feels huge.

"Thank you, Papa." Molly gives him a big hug.

Papa grabs ahold of her and hugs back. He holds her tightly in his arms as if he will never let go. Her cheeks flare with happiness and comfort. She is home and surrounded by her loved ones. Instead of muting her voice, even more, he magnifies it. Nobody has ever done that for Molly.

"Of course," Papa replies with a comforting smile. "Let's get back to the cake so we can have it finished by the time she gets here."

"Ok." Molly tastes some of the cake batter.

"How does it taste?"

"Delicious!" she says with a smile. The cocoa fills her taste buds and makes her mouth water even more.

"Ok, now we have to pour it into a cake pan and bake it," Papa says, reaching for the cake pan. "I'll tilt the bowl, can you scrape out the batter?"

"Yep, I got it." Molly grabs her mixing spoon and begins to scrape the edges of the bowl. She leaves some batter in the bowl for her to eat later.

"Alright, now let's set the oven to 350 degrees." Papa sets the cake into the oven and sets a timer.

Molly is already eating the leftover batter. Papa laughs as he sees her getting into the leftover batter.

Her face is covered in chocolate batter. Her hands are covered in its residue. A smell of sugary chocolate comes off her.

Papa looks upon the mess, "Let's go clean you up." he giggles out.

"Why, I'm not finished." Molly licks the last bit of batter. "Ok, now I am."

"Ok, head upstairs and I will be up when I am done cleaning this mess." Papa starts cleaning up the scattered ingredients.

Molly walks up the stairs, carefully so she doesn't get chocolate on anything. Her hands are covered in cake ingredients and batter.

She approaches the bathroom.

"Oh my goodness, what happened to you," Nana asks.

"I ate cake batter," Molly replies.

Nana giggles, "Alright let's get you cleaned up."

Molly gets herself clean of the chocolate batter and puts a new pair of clothes on.

"Nana, can you put my hair in ponytails?" Molly asks, walking from out of her closet.

"Yes, I can put them in pigtails. Come here and sit on the stool."

Molly sits on the plastic bathroom stool as her grandmother brushed her hair. Her hair is put into two ponytails, split by her centered part. A ribbon hangs from each ponytail, hanging down along with her reddish-brown hair.

She looks into the mirror and takes a deep breath. She looks deep into her own eyes reflection. A shiver fills her body. Her gut wrenches in fear. Why is she feeling such an intense fear? And how is she fearing something when she is home?

"The social worker should be here shortly. Let's go prepare your cake." Nana interrupts Molly's thoughts.

She stands there for a moment and tries to understand what is going on.

*It's probably nothing.* Molly tries to convince herself.

"Ok, coming." she ignores it and runs down the stairs.

Molly enters the kitchen.

Papa takes the cake out of the oven, "It will need time to cool, but we can make the frosting while we wait." he says.

"Ok." Molly walks over to help her grandfather.

They start the process of making the frosting. Molly is excited to use the mixer again. Hopefully this time it doesn't fly everywhere.

Time flies by as they make the wonderful chocolate frosting to top off the thunder cake. Moments after they finish a knock hits the front door.

"I will get it," Molly says, running to the front entry before her grandparents can respond.

She opens the door to a woman standing on the welcome matt.

"Why hello, aren't you cute." the woman says.

"Hi, are you the social worker lady?" Molly asks.

"Yes, I am. My name is Marley" the woman smiles in an attempt to comfort Molly.

"Hi Marley, come on in," Papa says from behind Molly.

The woman walks in.

Marley is a tall lady, with a beautiful complexion, and gorgeous black hair. Molly is in complete awe.

Thunder cracks throughout the sky, a shiver settles deep into Molly's gut. She is frightened by all of the emotions.

She closes the door. Resting her body up against the door, she takes a deep breath and tries to forget about all of the emotions the day has brought on so far.

She follows the adults as they walk into the kitchen.

"Go ahead and take a seat at the kitchen table, Molly and I made you thunder cake. Would you like a piece?" Papa asks the women.

"Yes please, thank you very much," Marley replies.

"Molly, can you help me frost the cake?" Papa says walking towards the cake.

"Yep." Molly comes trotting in.

"Good thing you got here safely, it's raining hard out there." Papa begins spreading the frosting.

"Yeah, it was fine. It is raining harder up here than it is in Orsus." Marley replies.

Nana sits down at the table by Marley and they begin talking.

Together Molly and her grandfather spread the frosting along the cake's surface. Nana and Marley continue talking about something, but Molly can not tell what they are saying. She hears something about her Mom, and her heart drops to the pit of her stomach.

*I'm sure it's fine, Mom is ok.* Molly's thoughts go to the worst, and she does her best to push the worries aside.

Molly continues to apply frosting on top of the chocolate cake. Papa smears a finger of frosting on her cheek. She giggles and wipes a little onto his face.

"Truce, I don't want to waste the frosting," Papa says, laughing along with Molly.

They clean themselves off with a dishrag. Once they are clean they gather a cutting utensil to cut the cake. Molly dries her hands off with a clean towel.

"I will grab the plates, can you grab the forks?" Papa says.

"Yeah, how many?" Molly replies.

"Four should be good." Papa continues to grab the plates and lay them out onto the countertop.

Molly grabs the forks from the drawer and lays them alongside the plates. "Here you go."

*~ Riley Brett ~*

"Great, now we need to dish out slices." Papa starts cutting the cake into pieces and dishes one onto each of the four plates. "Here you take two to the table and I will get the rest."

"Ok." Molly grabs ahold of two prepared plates and walks towards the table.

As she gets closer to the table she can hear the conversation more clearly.

"With her being clean and proving to the government she is stable. We are going to give her another chance with Molly. Molly is going back with her mother." Marley says.

Molly drops the plates.

Her heart stops and breaks itself into trembling pieces.

Glass spreads across the floor and around her feet.

Her eyes begin to prickle.

*Go back?* Molly's thoughts explode in confusion and fear. *Why? Will he be there?*

Everything fades out, all she can hear is her inner thoughts, and her heart beating irregularly fast. Her hands begin to sweat.

*Go back?* Her happiness wanes into the past. Fear and anger crawl through her bloodstream. The thought of leaving her *home* makes her sick to her stomach. Leaving her safety and comfort behind.

*Go back?* She shivers in disbelief. All the memories flood in. Every night she would lay in bed awake because the fear wedged her eyelids open. All of the beatings she had watched her mother go through. The near-death her mother reached every time. How could she possibly go back to that?

Thunder crackles from outside and rattles the home.
*I can't go back.*

## Section 2

# 7 years and a forceful smile

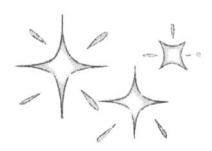

## Chapter 1

# Fabricated Vows

Rough carpet spreads beneath Molly's feet as she runs downstairs. The air is full of scent coming from burning candles'. Candles' are sitting all around the house, one almost on every countertop. Her skin warms as the heater finally kicks in, the cool air only sits by the windows now.

Molly sits down on the couch next to her mother.

"Hey sweetie." her mother says.

"Hey," Molly replies, crossing her legs.

She moved in with her mother after the social worker came, Jen had rented a duplex in a town called Caput, across the bridge from Orsus, an apartment for just the two of them. After Marley broke the news to Molly and her grandparents, Molly had to pack her bags and get ready to go back with her mother.

~ Riley Brett ~

What happened after that is what hurt Molly so badly.

Marley had mentioned that Nocens was in jail still, little did any of them know he had been out for a week before she had made that statement. Molly got back with her mother and shortly after, he came back. He abused Jen upon the basement floors, the upstairs, and in their bedroom on the 3rd floor, causing screams to echo throughout the house. Molly made many prayers to whoever was listening, she begged for mercy as she leaned on her knees. The sound of her mother's body being slammed around is now forever imprinted into her head. No matter how hard she tries to get the sound to stop repeating, it doesn't work. It haunts her in her nightmares and flashes through her mind during midday tasks. There is nothing she can do to escape it, except for one thing. Soccer.

Molly started playing soccer when she was four, but not until recently was she able to really get into it. The second she steps onto the field, every scream and every chill along her skin fades into nothing. She is free of the heart-wrenching memories. As she ties her cleats and pulls her sock over her sweaty shin guard, a feeling of relief and safety floods over her. On the field, she can be whoever she wishes to be, without the restriction of pain. She can use the pain to push her farther into the sport, and that, that passion from within, drives her to become the best version of herself she could possibly be.

After a huge fight 2 months ago between Nocens and Jen, Nocens moved 4 hours out of town. The fight was so big, Molly was sure her mother wouldn't make it. . .

*Jen's scream travels throughout the house. "Molly! Get outside."*

*Tears pour down Molly's cheeks. Her entire body trembles from deep within her nerves, her skin shakes with fear. She runs outside the first chance she gets.*

*She stands upon the dark green grass and smells the late fall sent. The sky is almost pitch black, the only light is coming from the moon and glitching streetlights.*

*Screams come from inside the house.*

*"No!" Molly yells, falling to her knees. "Mom!"*

*A twist makes its way down her neck and spine.*

*Jen comes running out and pulls Molly along with her." Come on we have to go." her mother says weakly.*

*They get into the car and make plans for the night when Jen realizes she left her purse inside.*

*"I need to go get my purse," Jen says.*

*"Mom no! You can't, what if he kills you? You can't die, mom please don't" Molly Beggs.*

*"It will be fine. Here, do you know how to call 911?" Jen sets her phone on the center console.*

*"No. Mom, please don't go," she begs weakly.*

*"Here is the dial pad. If I don't come out shortly, dial 911. Ok?" Jen looks into Molly's eyes.*

*"Ok. . . be careful." tears slip down Molly's cheeks.*

*Jen gets out of the car and runs back inside. Leaving Molly alone and frightened.*

*The warm car air fills her lungs. Every second goes by like an hour. The muscles along her arms and fingers are tense and ready to dial. She stares at the house door, waiting for her mother to make it out. Her face is soaked with fearful tears.*

*She leans over the phone, praying her mom will make it out alive. More everlasting seconds go by, still, she is nowhere to be seen. Molly dials the numbers and waits.*

*A clash comes from inside the house. Seconds later a scream travels through the damaged air.*

*"Mom!" Molly yells.*

*The door opens and slams. Her mother comes running out with her purse.*

*"Don't come back!" Nocens yells after Jen.*

*Jen gets into the car and releases a heavy breath.*

*"We're staying at a hotel tonight." Jen manages to say.*

*After that Jen said she would never go back to him.*

. . .

The memory fades.

"How was your weekend with Nana and Papa?" her mother asks.

"It was good. Nana and I baked cookie bars. Then all of us watched the football game." Molly replies with a smile.

"That's good, I'll be right back. I'm going to get some food, want anything?" Jen says, walking into the kitchen.

"No thank you."

Molly twiddles her thumbs. Something shimmers from the corner of her eye. She looks over to the window and sees an odd picture reflect from off her mother's laptop. She walks over to the laptop and sees pictures all across the screen.

*Is that? No, it couldn't be. She promised.* Molly feels her face flush.

Pictures of a Jen and Nocens getting married.

Molly scrolls down, looking at all of the pictures. A sickening feeling fills her stomach.

*They couldn't have. Could they?* Molly wonders.

She watches all of the pictures flash before her eyes. Her throat tightens.

Jen walks back into the room, chewing on some food.

"What is this?" Molly manages to ask, getting up off the couch.

Jen sits down next to the laptop. She looks up and smiles, "Aren't you happy?"

Molly is speechless. She stands there in the middle of the living room, trying to find words to describe how she is feeling.

*Happy? Why would I be happy?* Molly thinks. *There is no escaping this. I told her how I feel yet she doesn't care.*

"Yeah . . ." Molly says under her breath, holding in all of the tears pressing against her eyes.

"We got married this past weekend, in Vegas. Isn't that so cool? Aren't you so happy for me?" her mother replies with a sudden burst of excitement.

Molly's heart drops. Fear threatens her eyes.

"Yeah, so happy," Molly says, this time forcing herself to smile.

"I knew you would be!" Jen hugs Molly.

Molly feels a sense of resentment towards her mother. Jen squeezes tight enough for the both of them. Her body still so thin, with such fair skin.

Memories flash into Molly's head. Times when Jen would pick her up from school in her work uniform. Looking beautiful, Molly was convinced her mother was the prettiest girl she has ever seen. The way her thick hair flowed and was tied into a ponytail. Or how her makeup was applied so perfectly, magnifying the green from within her eyes. Molly wished she could grow up to look exactly like her mother. But now? Now it's different. Jen looks weak again. Thin, and unhealthy. Molly can't help but wonder what is going on with her mother.

"Do you want to order Chinese food to celebrate?" Jen asks. Pulling Molly away from the memory.

"Sure," Molly replies, trying to keep a smile on her face.

"Ok, I will call and order," Jen says, walking away.

Molly sits back down onto the couch and scrolls through the photos again. Trying to understand how this could have happened. He was gone. For good. How did they go from not speaking to getting married?

Unless they were talking the whole time...

She studies the photos. Every speck upon the screen. Wondering how they were able to smile so wide, fake so well. After everything he did to her, she married him.

*I wonder what vows they made to each other? Or what lies they created. How many promises did they make to one another that they may never keep?* Molly wonders.

Jen comes walking back into the room. "Ok, they should be on their way shortly," her mother says.

"Ok," Molly replies, forcing herself to act as if she doesn't mind.

"Oh, and I have more news." a smile spreads across Jen's face.

"Oh yay," Molly says sarcastically.

"So, you know how Noc lives up in Metus?"

"Yeah . . ." Molly's heart drops, splashing fear throughout her stomach.

"Well, we are going to be moving in with him!" Jen says excitedly. Her smile widening between her bright red cheeks.

Molly feels light-headed. Her hands shake and sweat. She sits down and forces a smile, though it only comes off as a leer.

"Are you alright? You look sick." Jen studies Molly's face.

"Yeah, no I'm fine. I am just so happy." Molly pulls herself together, feeling all of the pain sink deep into her stomach. Trying to make it disappear. No matter what pain she is feeling she wants her mother to be happy, and if this makes her happy then she will push herself through it.

"Ok, great. Me too. I am going to put on a movie, how's that sound?" Jen sets her laptop aside and grabs a disk from the DVD holder.

"Yeah." Molly can't manage herself to say much more than a one-word response.

Jen puts a movie into the DVD player and turns the TV on.

Everything fades out, her emotions turn numb. She fights the feeling, but it sinks despite her fight.

She takes a deep breath and tries to feel the air consume her lungs.

## ~ Riley Brett ~

*It will be ok, I know it will. There is more to life, there are beautiful things out in the world. I just have to keep fighting in order to see it all.* Molly reminds herself of the positive things to look at. *There is always a light.*

Ignoring the hopeless feeling she grabs onto the happy thoughts and the amazing memories. Especially the ones with T (Tutela, T for short). T is Molly's best friend, they spend practically every single day together.

Molly met T when she first moved in from her grandparent's house when she was 5. T lives across the alley from Molly, so it is very easy for them to hang out.

T goes through everything with Molly. She makes Molly feel like she can be a kid. Without T, Molly wouldn't be able to feel that or make the amazing memories they have together. They have sleepovers almost every night, except for school nights. They play all kinds of fun games; they jump on the trampoline, they play kitchen, they play school and all kinds of imaginary games.

Whatever Molly goes through, T is right by her side, ready to comfort her and help her through every step. Same with T, whatever happens to T, Molly has her back through anything and everything.

A loud sound comes from the TV. The memories with T disappear and Molly glides into a numbness. She has no idea how to feel or what to say, she is completely speechless. She fights all of the horrible memories of him being around. But it's no use, they break through and release worry throughout her mind.

Jen continues to talk, though Molly receives it all in a blur.

Multiple questions run through her head, she can't find the strength to ask any of them.

Molly lays along the couch staring up at the ceiling, trying to sort her thoughts and questions. Suddenly a knock hits the door. She pops up.

"I'll get it, it's probably the Chinese food," Jen says, walking to the main door.

Molly continues to let her eyes travel along the ceiling, inspecting its bumpy surface. A question floats upon her mind, one that needs to be answered. Hopefully, she can must up the strength to ask it.

Her mother comes back into the living room with the food and a couple of paper plates.

"Here you go," Jen says, handing Molly a plate and a plastic fork.

"Thanks." Molly grabs onto the plate.

"Dish out whatever you'd like." Jen opens the delivery bag and pulls out the food.

Molly begins dishing out food onto her plate, still a question lingering through her mind. She begins to eat, trying to come up with a way to ask the question.

"So, are you excited? I heard there is a school right down the street and there are nice kids in the apartment complex we will be staying in." Jen says, a smile imprinted onto her face.

"Yeah. . ." now is her chance. "I have a question." Molly continues nervously.

"Ok?"

"When do we move?" Molly's body tenses up, fearing the words that may come out of her mother's mouth.

"This week actually, we should be fully moved out by the end of the month," Jen replies, more excitement radiating off of her.

Her muscles tense up throughout her entire body. Molly can feel the fear lay within her poked up arm hairs. Her mind aches with confusion, "What . . .?" she stutters.

"Yep, we have it all planned out. You will finish the month off at your school now, then you will transfer to one of the schools in Metus. I actually already started to pack, all that is left is your things and the furniture." Jen continues to chew her egg roll.

*A month? This can not be true. How could this happen? We were doing so well, or so I thought. Was she going to tell me if I didn't find out? Or would she wait until the last minute?* Molly's mind continues to dwell on the frightening news.

Everything fades out, shortly the evening turns into the nighttime. Molly fell into an autopilot, the world became a blur, besides the thoughts flashing through her mind.

Molly looks outside, nothing but a dark sky fills her site. Cars race down the busy road, bright lights shining in front of them. She takes on the site and begins to feel sleepy. A yawn releases from her body and makes its way into the air.

Jen is asleep on the couch with the movie still playing. Molly feels the stress crawl back, she takes herself upstairs and into her room. There she lays in bed, staring at the colorful colors that fill her room.

*Why are we the ones that have to move in with him? Four hours from everyone we know, what does he plan to do with us? Or better yet, to us?* The questions reappear in Molly's mind.

She tries to calm herself, but nothing seems to do the job. Instead of repeatedly taking deep breaths, she walks over to her window and takes a seat aside from it. Her eyes wander through the darkness of the night, she spots a street light and stares upon its shimmering light. She lets her eyelids fall freely, tears drip upon her cheeks. Releasing pain from deep inside her body. Fear prickles along her soft, fair skin.

Now that Molly is 7 she knows more of what to expect, but this. This was far from expected.

*Is this what it will always be like? Is this what life is really like?* Molly wonders. *Movies sure amp it up.* She rests her head upon her hand, "I hope there is more to life." she whispers into the silence of the dark and lonely house.

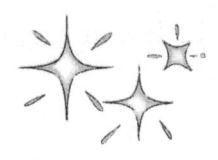

## Chapter 2

# Racing Raindrops

The next few weeks go by fast, too fast. Molly watches the house pack up with ease, all into boxes and bags. Leaving the house look so empty, it's hard to tell anyone had even been there. She feels her heartache as the day gets closer and closer. Saying her goodbyes to all of her friends and teachers, leaving her with a painful whole.

She feels the weeks fade into the past as she wakes up on moving day. Her heart drops into her stomach, her nerves are tense and confused. Fear has layered every inch of her body, making it hard to feel or think of anything else.

Four hours. Four hours from everyone Molly and her mother know. Just each other, and him. Him. The one who threw Jen down the stairs and hit upon her body without a speck of regret or mercy. The one who screamed out how worthless Jen is, but that isn't the worst part. The craziest part is, Jen thinks she deserves it and believes his despicable remarks.

Molly tries to wake her body by stretching, it does no good. Her nights are restless due to the countless nightmares. They have been happening ever since she can remember. Waking up the day after she can remember them so vividly, sometimes she can even remember them for years.

She looks around her empty room and tries to push the worry aside. Molly and her mother are driving there today with just the things in Jen's car. All the furniture is being left behind for Jen's friends who decided to take over the rent. Along with a few other things of theirs.

Molly gets herself ready for what she expects to be a long day. She gathers the last of her things and stuffs them into her backpack. The house smells like cleaning material and fresh candle scent. The walls are cleaned of all the art, and the carpet is freshly shampooed.

She brushes her teeth in the bathroom for what she assumes to be the last time. A dance breaks loose as she brushes along her teeth with the minty toothpaste. It reminds her of her grandparents and how much fun it is to be with them. How she can always go back to her grandparent's home. The one place that will always welcome her with warm arms. *I miss them.*

Molly pushes the thought away before she starts to shed tears. She moves on and brushes her hair.

"Molly, are you almost ready?" her mother yells from downstairs.

"Yeah," Molly replies, continuing to brush out last night's snarls.

She grabs her backpack and begins to exit the room. Standing at her bedroom doorway she feels a rush of fear and sadness, "Goodbye." she whispers.

Molly slowly makes her way down the stairs, taking in the last few moments she has left in the house. She may never see it again. Not only that, but she is having to leave all of her cheerful moments. Especially the ones with T, Molly will miss her the most.

She walks along the rough carpet, and feels its crust beneath her feet, for the last time. She breathes in the candle scent, trying to hold onto it for as long as possible.

Finally, she feels ready and leaves out of the side door. Being the last step she will ever take in the house, for all she knows.

She runs along the crooked sidewalk and into the car. Snacks are organized in the back seat, prepared for the long car ride. Molly stuffs her bag beneath her feet, then wraps herself with her fluffy blanket. She feels the warmth from within the car lay along her body, escaping the cold Caput air.

The duplex Jen had rented was right across the Orsus town border, entering into the small town of Caput.

Molly gathers her coloring book and her colored crayons, trying to prepare herself for the long car ride they are about to encounter.

"Ready?" her mother asks, peeking her head into the car from the open driver's side door.

"Yep," Molly replies quietly. *Ready as I'll ever be. . .* her mind admits.

Jen finishes her cigarette and hops into the car. "Alright, let's get on the road."

Molly feels her body jerk as the car pulls out of the parking spot. Her gut wrenches, causing her stomach to twist uncomfortably. She ignores it and proceeds to color.

They begin their four-hour journey along the road. Jen listens to the radio up front, tuning in and out of stations as they pass through small towns. The drive is mostly surrounded by fields of food and widespread grassland.

"This will be so good for us!" Jen says, turning down the radio.

The comment catches Molly's attention.

"It will be our chance for a fresh start. Getting to know more people. Seeing new things and exploring new places!" her mother continues excitedly.

A piece of hope flares inside of Molly. She tries her best to not let hope consume her, but it might be too late.

"Yeah." Molly agrees. "It seems kind of weird to me that he is moving us four hours away from everyone we know. Don't you think?" she finally says what is on her mind.

"No, I think it will be fine. This will be a good way to get out there. We have never been here before, there will be so much to explore."

Molly thinks upon her mother's comment. *Maybe she is right. Maybe this will be good for us, and we can create a new life for ourselves. It will be fine.*

She lets hope override the negative worries.

Jen tunes into a radio station and a song fills the air.

Molly lets the music fill her ears, and make her body bounce due to the base. She feels the song and listens to her mother sing along. Sparks of hope fill her mind, maybe it will all work out after all?

Each town they pass has a water tower, everyone being a different color or design. Sometimes even both. Molly watches for them as they drive by or through towns. She likes the variety of color or creative differences between towns and their water towers'. Some are plain white with bold lettering, and others are colorful from top to bottom.

When Molly and her grandparents went on long car rides they would do the same. They would search for water towers in every town they would come by. Now that Molly is without them, she wants to continue the game, even if it is by herself.

When there is nothing but grass on site, Molly stares deep into the sky. Imagining dreams so bright, it shows her a light. She may not understand now, but later it may be dark enough to see the light's true glimmer.

The sky contains nothing but thick grey clouds, yet, Molly finds a way to create stories and passionate goals. No solid color is strong enough to stop a dreamer from seeing their true potential. And it has never seemed to stop Molly.

Her eyes explore the clouds, searching for a speck of blue along the ever so dark sky. Shortly rain begins to fall along the car windows', not a dot of blue within the dark sky. Molly transfers her stare over to the racing raindrops, reminding her of the times she would watch the rain when she was little. Staring out the window she watches the huge droplets bounce against the glass. Gliding down the clear panel as it collides. The larger droplets travel faster and eventually consume the smaller ones. She watches the water travel down the clear glass until they begin to dry.

Molly is reminded of all the long car rides she would go on with her grandparents. All the stories they would tell, all the songs they would sing. Most importantly singing along to "You Are My Sunshine." by Johnny Cash. The lyrics repeat themselves over and over again in her head, pictures flash throughout her mind. The wonderful memories with her grandparents come flooding back. Making her eyes sting at the thought of being so far away from them. She pushes the memories aside and tries to distract herself.

"Are we almost there?" Molly asks. Not knowing if she wants to get there faster or slow the time.

"Yes, we are an hour away," her mother replies.

Butterflies fly around Molly's stomach. They fly in fear, making her feel sick.

She shoves snacks into her mouth, trying her very best to stay calm and act as if none of it bothers her. But you can only fake for so long . . .

"Are you hungry?" Jen asks, watching Molly eat all of the snacks.

"No, I'm ok," Molly replies, forgetting about all of the food she had just eaten.

"Are you sure, because you just ate half of the snacks?" Jen raises a brow.

"Oh right, um yeah I am hungry. Really hungry." Molly does her best to hide her emotions.

"Why didn't you say so? We can stop and get food at the next exit."

"Ok, thanks." her hidden emotions crawl beneath her skin, itching at a way out. Molly has never been a great liar. She doesn't want to lie but she has tried to tell her mother how she feels and it has never seemed to matter. She feels as if her emotions will never be valid in the eyes of her mother. That hurts Molly beyond words. She can scream, she can write, she can run, but no matter what, she does not feel heard. Her voice is always shoved aside into a pile of irrelevance. She finds it easiest to stay silent, though she has her moments of braveness. There are times when things get so horrendous she cannot live with herself if she didn't speak up, she only wishes she could always have that bravery.

"Why don't we stop at the grocery store so that I can buy some food to make dinner. You can get something there." her mother says.

"Ok, what are we having?" Molly asks.

"Barbecue ribs and corn. How's that sound?" Jen looks at Molly through the rearview mirror.

"Yeah, that sounds good!"

"I know they're your favorite." Jen smiles, giving a glimpse of her shiny white teeth.

They pull off of the highway onto the exit. There they retrieve items for dinner; Baked beans, corn, ribs, barbecue sauce, chips, and Nocens's favorite iced tea. Molly can feel her tummy rumble with excitement to eat all of the delicious food. She gets a few snacks from the store to hold her over until dinner. The grocery store trip only takes thirty minutes, they are on a time crunch to get to the apartment before Nocens does so that dinner is ready.

Shortly they are able to get back on the road and finish their road trip. Her mother speeds most of the way in order to make it there quickly, Jen wants to surprise Nocens with dinner when he gets back from work.

Along the way, they notice the sky getting darker and the air picking up with strong wind. Luck would have it they get caught up on red lights, slowing them even more.

Molly watches the scenery pass by in a flash. Examining all of the different stores and homes, trying to get a feel for the area. The dark grey sky weakens the scenery, making everything look somber. She hopes this isn't what it will always look like.

As they reach the parking lot of their new *home*, Molly feels hope spike her mood. Here it isn't as dark, there are kids playing around in the snow. There are people shoveling, walking their dog, and even people building snow forts. A smile wrinkles her face.

*A fresh start.* Molly takes a deep breath, looking along the building's rough brick walls. *This will be good, it will be fine. Mom said he's changed plus we have neighbors all around us, I doubt anything will happen like before.*

~ *Riley Brett* ~

"Here we are," Jen says, putting the car into park.

"It's bigger than I expected," Molly replies, pressing her face against the car window.

Molly grabs her things and gets out of the car. Breathing in the cold winter air, she feels the strong wind brush along her coat. She looks over to the side of the building and sees a large pile of snow, perfect for a snow fort.

"Molly, can you come help me carry things in?" Jen says, gathering food from the backseat.

"Yeah," Molly replies, walking back to the car.

Together they grab the groceries and make their way to the building's main door. There beside the door, a girl sits on the bench with a book gripped in her hands. Molly tilts her head in curiosity. She can't wait to make new friends, even though the thought of talking to strangers scares her. She runs through the door.

Inside the building, two staircases lead to different areas. One leads to the lower level apartments and the other leads to the higher level apartments. Molly follows her mother to the upper level, upon that level, there are 4 doors. Molly walks up the stairs, holding onto the railing nervously. She gulps at the worries entering her mind, *it'll be ok . . .it'll be ok. . .* her mother walks through the first door to their left, leaving it cracked for Molly. She stops at the top of the stairs, trying to calm herself before entering her new life. Her lungs shake with every breath, she breathes in through her nose, then out through her mouth. Trying her very best to steady her breathing. She begins to walk to the door when her gut wrenches. Her hand reaches for her side, trying to rid the uneasiness. She ignores the ache and carries forward, entering her new *home*.

Grey walls spread across the apartment, silver furniture lays along with the floors. She enters a living room that leads into a kitchen wrapping around the wall. Aside from the kitchen, a glass door opens up to a screened balcony. She makes her way over to the balcony and looks over the busy road. Across the street, there is a strip of businesses, along with a parking lot around the back and trees surrounding the buildings. As if they were trying to hide what lays beyond their large leaves.

"Isn't it nice?" Jen asks, standing alongside Molly.

"Yeah. . . I like the view." Molly replies. She has always wanted a balcony, the view of a street at night soothes her. The way the tall poled lights hang over the streets, making the road glow of limitless possibilities. All kinds of people going to different places, each having a unique story as to where they are going and why. The billions of differences, yet, all of the similarities. It fascinates her and only causes her curiosity to grow.

"I knew you'd like it." Jen smiles, looking beyond the glimmering glass.

Molly smiles, a bit of comfort settles her skin. Familiarity makes her feel safer than she thought she could feel.

"I am going to start dinner. Can you grab the rest of the things from the car and begin to unpack your room, it is the last room down the hall." Jen says, walking into the deep kitchen.

"Sure," Molly replies. She walks down the hallway and explores the carpeted apartment.

She looks along the empty walls. The walls have no sign of life, no sign of someone living here. She spreads her arm, letting her fingertips glide along the smooth wall. To the left, she notices a small bathroom, again grey. No sign of any color. Just grey and silver. To her right she spots a big bedroom, she peeks her head inside. A big bed takes up most of the room, along both sides of the bed a nightstand sits. She tilts her head in confusion, it's so clean. She closes the door as if she never entered.

Straight ahead two steps, a door rests cracked. She pushes the door open. A small room with a bunk bed to her left and a nightstand to her right. This room is different, it is just waiting to be colored and organized with all kinds of toys. She feels her future write itself along the room's walls. It is full of potential, the thoughts excite Molly.

Throughout the rest of the evening, Molly gathers the rest of their items from the car and brings them inside. She organizes her things perfectly in her new room, she can't think of much else while she arranges her things. Though the smell of delicious food filling the air, making her tummy rumble.

Molly walks into the kitchen, "How much longer until the food is done?" she asks.

"It is almost done. Notices should be here at any moment." Jen replies.

*Mom says he's changed, and he is a better man. I can't help but fear him and all he can do.* Molly reminds herself of what her mother told her before they came. *Mom seems excited, so I should be too. I want to see her happy, maybe he can do that. Maybe he can make her happy.*

Molly smiles back at her mother.

"Can you help me set the table?" Jen asks.

"Yeah," Molly replies, gathering a few plates and setting them on the table mats.

A creek comes from by the main door. Molly's gut twists and turns, she drops the fork she had grabbed from the drawer.

"Hi, Hunny," her mother says, greeting Nocens with a large hug.

Nocens picks her up, gripping along Jen's skinny body.

Molly picks up her fork and steadies her stance. After all of the built-up strength, his presence still weakens her.

Nocens walks over to the counter and sets his lunch box down. "Hi Moll." he smirks.

"Hi," Molly replies weakly.

"What is that smell, something smells burnt." Noc sits down at the table.

Jen rushes over to the food. "Yeah, the ribs got a little burnt. But they should still be good," she replies, still smiling.

Noc angrily looks her in the eye. "Can you do anything right?" he asks aggressively.

"Here it should be alright, I have some veggies and chips." Jen tries to keep her smile, placing food in front of Noc.

Molly sits down in front of her food. She takes a bite of the ribs and enjoys the wonderful taste of barbecue sauce.

Noc takes a small cautious bite. "I can't eat this. I'm going across the street to get some real food." Noc says, shoving his plate aside.

"I am sorry, I rushed to finish this meal for you so it could be done by the time you got home," Jen says slightly under her breath.

Noc walks to Jen's side." I'm sure this meat was expensive, no reason to waste it. Don't let it happen again." he replies aggressively, leaning over Jen.

"Ok, it won't happen again," Jen says weakly.

Noc grabs his wallet and storms out of the apartment. Slamming the door, making the walls tremble.

Molly looks over to her mom and watches Jen bury herself in her arms. Molly doesn't understand, the meal tasted fine to her. All she wants to do is make her mother feel better. The hope for her mother to be happy has quickly vanished.

"I think it tastes fine. . . I like it." Molly says, trying to comfort her mother.

Jen lifts her head out of her arms. "Thank you sweetie." she replies. Molly reads through her mother's fake smile.

*Why would he say that? It tastes fine. He was supposed to make her happier, she doesn't deserve this. How can I make her feel better?* Molly wonders.

Molly continues to chew her food.

"Before I forget, you are going with Nana and Papa for Christmas. Then you will come back here for new years." Jen says softly.

*~ Passion From Within ~*

Molly watches her mother slowly shift through the kitchen. Jen goes into her bedroom and closes the door.

Molly sits alone at the table, in a new empty life. She rests her head upon her hand and stares out the window, wondering what else the future has planned.

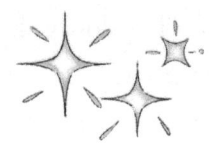

## Chapter 3

# Tears Upon A Blade

Molly spent the next few weeks at her new school. Trying so hard to make new friends and to fit in. She kept quiet throughout the school day, catching as little attention as possible. Her new school was so much different, it had confusing halls that led to many different rooms. The rules were hard to keep track of, all the different reasons to stay in a single file, and stop at every corner as her class walked down the halls. But most of all, the kids, they weren't very kind to Molly. Nobody tried to talk to her, though, she never tried talking to them. The thought of getting rejected by someone scared her, the thought of embarrassment made her uneasy, and worsed of all, getting teased made her second guess her existence.

Thankfully she is going to her grandparent's home for Christmas, which is in a few days but her mother thought it would be a good idea to go early.

Molly is in the car with her mother on their way to meet up with her grandparents. They had left right after school, Molly had her bag packed and ready to go. She can't wait to get away from all of the new chaos of moving and "getting a fresh start". Besides the moving, Jen and Nocens had been fighting here and there. The yelling traveled through the new apartment walls just as easily as they did back *home*. Well, Jen's old duplex.

So far it has only been verbal fighting, to Molly it almost seemed worse. The verbal threats and hatred, caused Molly to wonder if it was normal to fight so constantly and horribly cruel. It is not normal, but how would she know, this way of life is all she has ever known.

Some nights she just shoves her head into her pillow and forces herself to sleep through it. It never seems to work like that, she barely sleeps. If it isn't the arguing keeping her up, it is the nightmares and the worries of missing her friends and family. Especialy T. How is she supposed to get through all of this without T? She lets out a sigh whenever she thinks about T, and her brother Lil Sam. She misses them. Along with the majority of the nights, she cries herself to sleep from the pain of missing everyone she knows and loves.

All she can do at this point is be thankful the fighting hasn't gotten physical, *yet*.

All she can do is look forward to the time with her grandparents.

Molly switches cars about 3 hours into the ride. Her Papa picks her up at the agreed meeting spot and welcomes Molly with a big hug.

She looks out of the window of her grandfather's truck and watches the snow caught along in the winds strong whistle. The sky is grey again, it has been grey a lot lately. Molly can't tell if it is just her noticing it because things have been rough lately or if it is just the winter gloom.

The sun peeks out from behind a huge grey cloud, making little shining paths along the road and tree lines. She watches the light spread across the earth's surface, and slowly cover itself back up.

She hangs her head in a state of sadness and curiosity. The sky seems to be reflecting her mood, *not possible.*

". . . you are my sunshine, my only sunshine. You make me happyyy when skies are greyyy, you'll never know dear how much I love you– . . ." Papa sings.

". . .please, don't take my sunshine awayyy. . ." Molly sings along with him. He looks back at Molly from the driver's seat for a split second and smiles into her big hazel eyes. The smile seemed to have lasted for much longer than just a second in Molly's mind, her cheeks glow with comfort and appreciation. His smile is contagious, it could make a whole room of depressed somber people smile bigger than they ever thought was possible. And boy did it ever make Molly smile, she couldn't help but feel the positivity from his presence.

She continued to watch the small towns pass by in a blur, all the way *home*. They pulled up the loose gravel road until they reached their driveway, turning up to a beautiful home placed amongst trees and bushes.

"Here we are," Papa says, turning off the truck.

*Home.* Molly took her time to admire the home. She scans the snow along the driveway edges, spotting for snow fort spots. None of the snowbanks are tall enough for the fort she wishes to make, but it doesn't take a speck of happiness from her face.

She hurries out of the car and runs into the house, through the garage door. Running so fast she runs into her grandmother and greets her with a great big hug.

Her seven-year-old body squeezes her grandmother until her arms begin to tire.

"Hi, sweetie. How was the ride up?" her nana asks.

"Hi." Molly enjoys the last few seconds of their hug. "It was good, longer than usual," she replies.

"I bet, it is 4 more hours than before. I am sure that adds a little bit." Nana smiles, kissing Molly's forehead. "I missed you."

"I missed you too," Molly speaks into her grandmother's arms, fighting the tears.

"Are you hungry?" Nana asks, releasing Molly from her tight hug. A common question her grandmother asks.

"Yeah." She follows her grandmother into the kitchen, and they enjoy an afternoon snack. All three of them. Together again. As if Molly had not left them after Marley broke the news. The news. . .

Everything changed after that one conversation. Everything.

Molly's world turned into something she could have never prepared herself for. A place where she had nothing but harmful curiosity, fear, sadness, and disbelief.

She never fully understood what was going on when it happened. She could never tell whether it was normal or not. Whether it was the world's normal or not, never fully realizing that it was her inevitable normal. She eventually learned how to deal with not knowing, she found a certain comfort in the uncomfortable. But the kids, the kids make everything different. In her "new life" she could deal with the *home* things (barely), but the kids at school. That is a whole other story. It's inescapable. The thought tugs at her gut. Creates an ache in her heart. Pressure in her eyes. And worst of all, pain upon her mind.

Molly never thought about the mental things, she only ever had to worry about the physicality. Now it's different. Now she has to fight more than just her own thoughts, she has to fight against other kid's words. It was a whole other kind of pain.

So unfamiliar.

So hurtful.

It all tore at her mind, making her ever so unstable.

She began to have thoughts. More scary than usual. Kinds of thoughts she didn't want to have. Thoughts that scared her far beyond words could explain. But the crazy part is, it is her own thoughts that are beginning to scare her the most.

These thoughts crawled along her brain, *every day*. Some days she was lucky to escape them for just a little while. But only a little while. And it was rare, it was hard to distract her mind from the haunting thoughts.

Oh, the thoughts. The way they crept upon her mind suddenly. So suddenly. At moments she would even jump or tremble.

They itch and scratch away at her, making her feel crazy. Absolutely crazy. She hadn't felt like herself for so long now, she is worried she will never be able to go back. To avenge who she once was. Who she even wished to be.

The memories of the words the kids had said or the words he had said to her.

He.

Nocens. The words he said to her.

Her.

Jen. The way she let his words travel into her ears. How she had listened.

All of it, down to every last sound wave. Everything taunted Molly, throughout each and every day. What does one do with the memories? One cannot throw them away, nor ignore them. How do you persevere through it all?

She wonders what to do, how to get rid of them. Not just them, but the pain that layers them. The pain. The pain isn't all that bothers her of course, it is the voicelessness and loneliness. The way everyone silences her. It is deafening. Nobody ever listens to her, no matter what she says. Especially when she tells her mother, she is always answered with "that isn't what really happened". Really? *"Was she not there?"* Molly always wondered.

Molly didn't give much thought to who she was telling these things to. Was she even telling the right people? Who was there to tell?

Nana finishes her snack and walks her plate into the kitchen, "Are you almost done Molly?" she asks.

Molly breaks loose of her deep thoughts. "Yeah, thank you," she replies with a smile.

"I have to stop by the office to pick something up before the holidays. I will be back soon, I just have to grab a folder I forgot yesterday." Papa says.

"Sounds good, I love you," Nana replies, kissing him on the cheek.

They exchange a rosy-cheeked smile.

"Bye Papa," Molly yells out as Papa exits through the garage door.

"Bye Molly, see you soon."

Molly smiles. She watches the door close behind him, and her smile slowly fades.

"Alright. I am going to go fill the bird feeders before I start dinner. Will you be ok?" her nana asks.

"Yeah, I'll be fine." Molly laughs. "You'll be right outside the door, I think I can manage."

"Ok sweetie, yell if you need anything." Fidum walks into the attached garage.

"Ok . . ."

*~ Passion From Within ~*

She feels the emptiness of the home shiver up her skin. Looking around, still the same home. But it feels different. What could it be?

Molly gets out of her chair and walks to the couch. She turns the TV on and switches between multiple channels. Until she realizes there is nothing good to watch and turns it off.

She sits on the cool leather couch. Tilting her head towards the large window beside the couch, opening up to the front yard. Still, the day is gloomy, not as gloomy as it was earlier but not much better either.

Her head falls on top of her hand, she props it up, watching the branches blow within the wind. Flashes erode her mind. . .

. . .

Deep screams fill her ears.
Loneliness consumes her skin.
The laughing kids crowd her vision.
Tears slide down to her lips, slowly filling her mouth.
Men's cologne floats upon the air.

. . .

Molly grabs her head, trying to shake the remaining memories. Her skin trembles with discomfort and confusion. Pain engraves itself within her stomach lining. Her mind consumed with fear and pain. The pain. Oh, it hurts.

. . .

Her throat aches tightly.
Screams fight through her body, trying to find a way out.
The room is dark and empty.

~ Riley Brett ~

The door is locked.

Cries travel through the walls.

Molly begs herself to find her bravery, but it is completely gone.

*Mom!* Her mind yells from within itself.

. . .

She pulls at her skin. *I can't do it anymore. I wish I could end it all.* Molly is now ripping along her trembling skin. *Please stop! It hurts!*

She rocks herself back and forth along the couch cushions. *How do I stop the pain?* Questions fill her mind as the pain strips her happiness down to a pile of nothing. *Go away!* She thinks hard, trying to think of a way to stop everything. To stop the pain.

She sits up. "I hate myself for thinking like this. I hate myself!" Molly quietly yells at herself. *Why do you think of such horrendous things?* Her mind thinks in confusion.

A thought pops its way into her head. She acts too quickly to even think through it. She ignores her mind cautioning her of the consequences. *If I do it in Grammy's room, nobody will ever know.*

Molly makes her way to the kitchen, she turns her head making sure it is clear and that nobody is here to see her.

She walks to the drawer beside the kitchen sink. Hovering over the open drawer she hesitates, her handshakes over the item. She forces herself to grab it, pushing away her morals.

Aside from the kitchen Grammy's bedroom sits, open and alone. Molly makes her way into the room and crawls into her sacred space. Just between the bed and the wall, a little space lays beside the nightstand. She settles herself in, cross-legged.

She rubs her thumb along the object, feeling its cool, rough edge. Guilt settles on top of her skin. *Don't think about it, it's fine.*

*I can't do it, I don't want to go back. I don't want to deal with the past. I don't want to deal with any of it. I just. . . I just can't.* More thoughts fill her mind, overcrowding what is already there. Pushing Molly over the final edge, she gives in.

She grips the handle and stares along the knife's silver surface. Watching her horrid reflection stare back at her. Tears slip down her face, dripping onto the shiny surface, bouncing back into the air. Her reflection blurs, she can't tell whether it is her eyes filling with tears or if it is the knife's shiny blade filling with water.

Sobs begin to weep from her body. Her shaky hand grips the handle even tighter until the anger blurs her mind. She pushes the sharp end of the butterknife along her fair skin. It isn't enough to make even a scratch.

Anger causes her shoulders to tense. *I hate this, I hate me. I want to kill myself, please just. . . just hurt me. I deserve it.*

She pushes as hard as she can along the skin of her left arm. Scratches form along her soft skin. *Why won't. . . it . . . do anything.* Her thoughts interrupt themselves with painful cries. She lets her head fall, dripping even more tears upon her lap. Driving a chill along her legs. *It isn't sharp enough. I need a real knife, a sharp knife.* Before she can do anything, the cries hold her captive to the secret spot tucked beside her Grammy's bed.

She tries her best to quiet down her cries. It feels wrong but oddly normal. Silencing her own self.

*It hurts so bad. Please make it stop. . .*

. . .

The rest of her stay with her grandparents goes by way too fast. Christmas morning went by especially fast, all of the laughs shared between them, all of the delicious Christmas cookies, everything they did went by in a flash. She feels herself glide through time, almost as if she had time traveled. She thinks back to her grandfather's words, "Time flies when you're having fun." he would always say with a little smile creasing his fragile skin.

She had known that for a while, but the older she gets, the faster time seems to go by. Her time spills into the living room of the new apartment in Metus, opening presents her mother had laying beneath the living room tree.

All she can remember from the ride home is the goodbye she had to say to both of them. It is always the most difficult part of leaving them. She always hugs them as tight as she possibly can, as if she will never see them again. In her mind, there is a constant worry of exactly that. The thought of never seeing them again, she can't even bear the pain, just thinking about it. The feeling of their tightly gripped hug stays along the surface of her skin. The smell of their home, *her home*, is still along her clothing. She doesn't want to take them off, ever.

The presents are perfectly wrapped. Every single one, with perfectly creased edges and tied ribbon. Molly almost doesn't want to rip it apart, *almost*.

Her mom grabs the camera and points it towards Molly, "Alright go ahead." she says.

Molly rips apart the paper on cue. Doll's clothes fall out of the paper, the ones Molly wanted. "Thank you mom!" she says, rushing over to hug her mother.

She hugs her mother tightly, releasing quickly. Realizing how skinny and weak her mother feels, *what's wrong with her skin, why is she so skinny?* She tries to hide the recognition of her mother's thin body. *Don't cry, don't say a thing.*

"You're welcome," Jen replies.

Jen's smile does not fool Molly for a second. She can tell when her mother is off and on edge. When she has lost more weight than her body could probably handle. But what would Molly do? What *could* she do? Call the police, and say what exactly? *Hey please help, my mother is freakishly skinny and seems off.* They would hang up quicker than they answered.

Just like any other time, she stays quiet.

"You forgot to thank a certain somebody," her mother whispers.

Molly tilts her head in confusion.

"He paid for it you know, you better thank him." Jen hisses through her teeth.

Molly isn't surprised by her mother's reaction. Noc is always the savior in her mother's eyes.

"Seriously." Molly says under her breath so Jen can't hear it. "Thank you Noc." she says as nicely as she can possibly manage. She wouldn't be surprised if she got yelled at for how she thanked him, it came off rather snotty than she had truly intended. It must be her reflex around him.

She gathers the wrapping paper from the gifts and puts it into a plastic bag.

"Thanks for cleaning up," Jen says, smiling.

*How can she do that? Act like everything is normal, and we are a happy little family.* Molly thinks. She can't tell why it bothers her so much. She is happy that they aren't fighting, but she isn't happy that they are so *perfectly happy.*

Molly takes her new gifts into her room and puts them into a pile with the ones from her grandparents. She is blessed with very nice gifts, anything she could want, she practically has. Well with an exception or two though *money can only by so much.*

She picks up an item from the pile and examines it, it is perfect. Brand new and waiting to be played with. Yet she felt emptier than she had before as if Christmas took more than it had given. How does that make sense?

She lets her legs fold and she sits along the carpet floor. She looks over all the colors, wondering which bright toy she will play with first. Alone in her room, she sits.

"Ah, stop." Jen giggles from the living room.

Molly jumps, any noise her mother makes, startles her. In every way, for every reason.

She turns back to her toys and plays with her brand new doll. It is a beautiful doll with straight blonde hair, blue eyes, and freckles across her button nose. The doll is dressed in a blue shirt and denim jeans.

Loneliness fills her room, wall to wall. Consuming her lungs, and flooding her bloodstream. Tears well in her eyes, she squeezes them shut, preventing them to slip. She squeezes her hands tightly, trying to alleviate the pain.

*It's fine. You're fine.* Molly tries to convince herself. *Why do I care so much?*

She drops her head down, thinking deeply upon her questions.

Tonight she goes to bed early. Playing with her toys can only do so much, after a while it gets repetitive and lonely.

She lays under her covers, staring at the dark ceiling. Her mind is clouded with too many thoughts and worries, she isn't able to focus on any of them specifically.

Her shoulder drops to the left, her body follows.

Voices louden from the other room.

She can't tell if it is fighting or just talking loudly. It sounds too aggressive to be just a loud conversation.

*Please not tonight. I can't tonight.* Molly prays from within her mind. *There's no use, nobody is listening. Nobody ever listens.*

Molly rolls to her right side and digs her head into her fluffy pillow. The darkroom calms her slightly, causing her tired eyes to give in to the exhaustion.

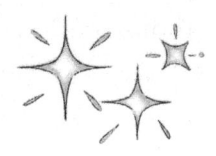

Chapter 4
=========

# This Isn't Love

Days roll by as if they were only minutes. Before Molly can tell, she is running around on New Year's Eve.

The apartment is full of something different, something other than the normal. Fresh pancakes were made for breakfast, and out of all things, the three of them watched a movie after lunch. Something so simple, but for them, so irregular. The last few days have consisted of such hope and happiness, Molly has given into the little game they had created. She came to realize, she would rather pretend to play their game rather than go out of her way to despise them and put her safety at risk. Plus, it was nice to not be so jumpy, even if it was just for a little while.

Despite all of the positivity, she still has worries. Along with nightmares here and there, and horrifying thoughts pop in every so often. Just taunting her, making sure she knows it is an imminent thing. Not thoughts of just the past, but the future too. It would never stop. No matter what. Molly feels it, she feels her little infinity form within her wrenching gut.

She accepts the inevitable and enjoys her blessings in the present.

"Would you like to help me make cookies?" her mother asks.

"Sure," Molly replies, walking into the kitchen.

"We're going to make snickerdoodles. Ok?"

"Sounds good."

Snickerdoodles are Molly and Jen's favorite.

The apartment smells like sugary cinnamon, making her mouth water impatiently. She can't wait to eat warm fresh cookies.

"Mom. I thought you didn't like cinnamon?" Molly asks.

"It's different in cookies. I don't mind it in cookies." Jen replies.

"Oh?" she doesn't want to admit how confused that comment makes her. Maybe she will understand it the more she thinks about it.

"Ok, they are almost done. Can you go wash up?"

"Yeah."

Molly makes her way to the bathroom down the hall and cleans off her sugar covered hands. Sugar sits in every crease of her damp skin.

She scrubs her hands free from all of the sugar speckles. Then rinsing her face, her mother had wiped some cookie dough along her rosy cheek. She didn't mind all that much, the dough tasted delightful.

After washing herself off, she makes her way back to the kitchen. Following the magnificent smell trailing through the air. *Mm cinnamon,* her mouth waters with excitement.

Jen takes out the cookie tray as Molly walks into the kitchen. She looks over the cookies, they are all stuck together. Instead of circular cookies, they are square and wide.

Molly giggles, "They're a little close, don't you think?" she says.

"Oh shush," her mother says laughing.

Molly laughs along with her mom, baking may not be her mother's hidden talent.

Jen cuts along the sides of each cookie, separating them from one another.

Before Jen can cut them all apart Molly grabs one from off the tray and gobbles it up.

"Hot!" Molly giggles.

"That's what you get for not waiting." Jen giggles along with her.

Despite the hotness of the cookie, Molly devours it within seconds. "Mm, nummy." she laughs.

"You little cookie monster!" Jen grabs onto her, holding her tight and tickling along Molly's most ticklish places.

"Ahh, mom!" she snickers, trying to fight the laughs.

Jen laughs, freeing Molly from the captive tickles.

Molly laughs even more, "At least the cookies taste good. I'll give you that." she says.

"Oh really?"

"Mhm." she snatches another and quickly leaves the kitchen, giving her mother a troublesome look while walking around the corner.

"You little stinker," her mother yells from the kitchen.

Molly plops onto the bottom bunk in her room, nibbling on the big square cookie. She lays on her back, letting her eyes travel along the bottom of the top bunk. Letting cookie crumbs fall along her baby face.

A loud crash comes from the kitchen, "Ah!" Jen yells.

"Mom!" Molly's heart drops. She drops her cookie and sprints into the kitchen.

"It's ok, I'm ok," Jen says, sitting along the floor. "I just dropped the cookie pan."

Molly crouches down to help her mother pick up the cookies. "You scared me." she genuinely looks into her mom's eyes.

"I'm fine sweetie." Jen tries to convince Molly. "Hey, I have an idea. Let's go sledding in the parking lot after dinner. We can have a little girls night." Jen smiles up at Molly.

"Ok. Yeah, I would like that" Molly replies, noticing her mother's forceful smile. *I wish she could know that she deserves better.*

The afternoon goes by quickly. Molly watches a few movies to pass some time. Before dinner, she sits by her window and watches the snowfall along the earth. Thinking of the statement "No snowflake is the exact same", *how is that possible?* She watches the sun lower beneath the far tree line, shining against each shimmery snowflake.

Snow piles up along the outer banks. She can only imagine how high the snow pile is alongside the building, the one she saw when she arrived here.

As soon as dinner is over, Molly quickly gathers her snow gear and runs outside.

The second she reaches the cold air, she feels her lungs freeze from the intake of frosty air. Snowflakes fall along with her coat, each flake having a beautiful shimmer.

*It's crazy that no snowflake is the exact same as all the others. Out of millions and billions, every single one has at least one difference.*

Snow falls along the top of her hat and slides down the surface of her slippery jacket. The street lights glow along the street, magnifying the falling snow.

*It is so beautiful.*

She runs along the fresh snow, sliding and slipping. Looking up into the dark night sky, peace fills the night. Even if it only lasts one night, she will take it, and she will take it for all that it is.

"Ready?" her mother asks, pulling a sled along her side.

"Of course!" Molly hops into the sled, bracing herself for the ride along the alley.

"Here we go!" Jen runs, trying her best to grip along the ground, but the mixture of snow and ice makes it almost impossible. But she runs on, slipping and sliding, She fights her way down the street, with Molly in the sled behind her sliding side to side and occasionally straight. "Hold on tight."

Molly grips onto the rope with her thick mittens. Cold flakes settle upon her face, cooling her cheeks and creating a rosy tone.

She grips tighter as the ride gets rougher.

At this moment, everything else fades. It is just her and her mom. Them and the mid-winter snow.

At this moment, everything feels ok. Happiness blocks every other thought. There are no memories flashing their way back into her head, no worries about what the future may hold.

At this moment, everything is safe. The happiness that spreads across her mother's face makes her feel at rest. As long as her mother is happy, she is most likely to be happy.

She only wishes this moment could last forever, but it is only a moment. . .

Jen tugs quickly left, Molly flies out of her sled. "Ahh!" Molly yells out, crashing into a snowbank along the alley.

"I'm sorry sweetie," Jen says, bent over with laughter.

Molly joins in with the laughter, despite the freezing snow that is dripping down her shirt.

"Come on, let's go get you warmed up." Jen grips onto Molly and rubs her hands along Molly's freezing body.

Molly feels the warmth of her mother heat the goosebumps that cover her chilled body. Snuggling in, she embraces the comfort her mother offers.

After cups and cups of hot chocolate, Molly makes her way to bed. Smiling ear to ear, it was a good day and she will forever hold onto it.

. . .

~ Riley Brett ~

New year's day comes close to its final hours.

Molly lays along the couch, snuggled up with her blanket waiting for midnight to hit.

Jen and Nocens walk in from smoking on the porch. Cigarette smoke fills the air as Jen walks past the couch.

Molly tries to focus on the TV, showing the New Year's countdown, still a few hours to go. She has no idea how she will be able to make it all the way until midnight.

Her focus leaves the TV, the apartment is full of tense air, more than usual. Discomfort sits along her skin.

Her tired legs don't want to leave the couch.

"Hey mom, can I sleep on the couch tonight," Molly asks, doubting her mother will say yes. She isn't allowed to sleep in the living room.

"Sure sweetie–" her mother replies.

Nocens looks over confused. "-No, she can't sleep out here," he says interrupting Jen's answer.

"Why not?" Jen asks, getting up in Noc's face.

"Because I say so," Nocens replies firmly, leaving the room.

"That isn't a good reason, c'mon it's New years. Don't be such a party killer."

The tension increases. Feeling as if the room is a bomb ready to explode.

"Mom it's fine, I don't need to sleep out here." Molly cuts in.

"No, you should be able to sleep out here," Jen says smiling.

The smile comes off odder than usual, Molly feels the difference.

## ~ Passion From Within ~

"I already said no, stop asking Jen," Nocens yells.

"She can sleep on the couch, it isn't a big deal," Jen yells back, smiling in his face.

"It's my house, I make the decisions. Don't overstep your boundaries," he says again, more firm and aggressively.

*It isn't a house.* Molly corrects him in her mind.

*Why is she pushing so hard, I said it is fine?*

"Get over yourself—"

"Leave then." He interrupts Jen, grabbing on to her.

-tick-

Molly trembles at the fighting. Not a day goes by where the fighting gets any easier, verbal, or physical.

"No, I don't have to."

*She really should not have said that.* Molly feels the bomb tick again, ready to go off any second. Take cover.

Molly runs into her room.

Yells continue down the halls.

-boom-

It explodes.

Bodies crash and fall. She covers her ears, trying to block out the sounds and prevent the chills.

She kicks her door shut, and packs her bag. *It's going to be a long night.*

Tears slip down her face, this time the tears don't break her they only sting and add to the future pain. The imminence of pain rides through her cool body.

Her arms are covered in tears, though she carries on.

*~ Riley Brett ~*

-crash-

Casualties have been affected. It is only a matter of time until it is over.

She flinches. Not one day. Not a single one can prepare her for the pain of the next.

The bag is packed and waiting on her bed, ready to go anywhere but here. She makes her way over to the window, watching the snowfall. Snow gathers along all of the earth's surface, shining from the bright street lights. She can imagine how it would feel, falling along her warm cheeks and melting as they make contact. Always wishing the flake would stay forever, they are too beautiful to part with. If only their beauty could last just a little while longer.

Tears splash along the windowsill. She drops her head, *please show me there is more to life. Please. . .*

-crash-

Yells come down the hallway.

"Molly let's go!" her mother says running into Molly's bedroom.

She lingers along the window, *let this peace come back to me.*

Molly grabs her bag and runs out of the room. Leaving everything else behind, never knowing if she will be back or leave forever.

She runs in front of her mother, watching her mother grab more than necessary.

*Really? Your makeup drawer.*

She cries, trying to leave as quickly as she possibly can.

"Mom!" Molly half begs. "C'mon, let's go."

"I'm coming," Jen replies, pulling all of her bags beside her.

Molly grabs some of her mother's bags and brings them down the hall.

"Oh I forgot something, go on. I'll be right behind you." Jen runs back up the stairs.

She can't stand here waiting while her mother runs back into all of that.

Walking up to the door she watches her mother rush around the corner smirking.

"Get out Jen!"

"Oh you're so intimidating," Jen says sarcastically.

Nocens walks closer to Jen. "If I ever see you again, *I will kill you.*" he says more aggressive than Molly has ever heard.

Her knees weaken at the thought. *Just looking at her, even in public?*

*He will kill her.* She tries to comprehend what had just been said.

There's no more time to think about it, they have to get out.

"Mom let's go!" Molly tries to pull her mom along with her.

Jen and her run down the stairs carrying all of their bags.

The bomb went off, but where is the *savior*?

Running out the door into an unpredictable future.

Molly lays in their hotel bed and watches cartoons streaming on the TV. Jen stepped outside to smoke a cigarette, but it has been 30 minutes since she left.

She worries about her mother, but there isn't much that she can do.

*So much for New years eve.*

Molly falls asleep to the TV, still no sign of her mother.

. . .

The bathroom fan wakes Molly from her deep sleep. Full of painful memories of the past and worries for the future.

She stretches her arms and wakes herself for the day to come. Last night's crazy turn of events has shaken her mind and has consumed her with confusion.

Despite the deep trembles, she pulls herself out of bed.

"Yeah, can you bring it?" Jen says from the bathroom.

"Mom?" Molly says, turning the corner.

Her mother is on the phone. Standing in the bathroom with a towel wrapped around her.

"-Yeah, hold on. Good morning, hey Noc found your DS. Would you like him to bring it?" Jen replies, holding the phone away from her face.

"My DS? Why would he come here just to bring me my DS?"

*We came here to get away from him. Now you want him to come and bring me my video games?* Molly thinks confusingly.

"Yeah. Why not?" Jen raises a brow as if she has no idea why Molly is so confused.

"Um, no I think I'm ok." she tilts her head in confusion.

*Why is she acting so weird?* Molly wonders.

"Really? Are you sure? I will just have him bring it since he is coming by anyway." Jen says, pulling the phone back to her face. "Yeah, could you bring the DS along with my makeup bag?" she continues on the phone, closing the bathroom door.

*He's coming here?* Molly's heart drops with fear. *I thought we came here to get away from him. . . he said he would kill her the next time he saw her. Is he going to kill her?* She worries about all of the frightening possibilities.

Her skin shakes, slowly going numb. There isn't anything that she can do. 4 years later and there still isn't anything that she can do, if anything she is even more voiceless. They are married now, together by law.

Cartoons continue on the tv. She sits down and hopes to be consumed by the tv's fictional tales, any story but her own.

It only lasts for so long, before her reality kicks back in and stings her throat. Ready to burst into tears at any moment.

But she can't give in, she can't cry. She would only be giving them the satisfaction of the pain they have caused her. Maybe if they saw the pain they would realize what horrible things they have actually done.

A knock hits the hotel door.

*Please be housekeeping.* Molly hopes.

"Molly get the door. It's Noc with your DS." Jen yells from the bathroom.

Her heart has now sunk, deeper than the pit of her stomach. *I said I didn't want it. Why is he here? He'll kill her.*

"Molly! Did you hear me?" Jen yells again.

Another knock hits the door. This time it is more like a pound.

"Yeah, I heard you," Molly says under her breath.

She walks over to the door and opens it slowly. The bathroom door directly to the left opens quickly.

Jen runs into Noc's arms, hugging tightly.

*What? Are you kidding me?* Molly cries on the inside. Holding it all in painfully.

Jen kisses Noc.

*Yeah, no I am done.* Tears fall down Molly's face. She quickly wipes them as they come down, trying to keep her composure and strength. *I will not let them get to me.* She states to herself.

Noc hands Molly a DS.

"Thank him, Molly." Jen snarls.

"Thanks," Molly says weakly, more tears glide along her warm face.

"Honey, what's wrong?"

*What's wrong? What's wrong? How could you not know what is wrong? EVERYTHING is wrong. Absolutely. . . everything.* More cries escape her body as thoughts fill her mind.

"Are you ok? You seem weird." Molly asks her mother.

"Yeah, I'm fine." Jen smiles in Molly's face, scarier than it is comforting.

"She's using," Noc says.

"Wha. . .what?" every inch of Molly's body trembles.

"Yeah she does drugs, she has been using her prescriptions more than she should be. So that she can get high. She has for a while now."

"No. She wouldn't." she looks up at her mother, noticing Jen's hesitation to deny it.

*He can't be right. That isn't true. She would never do anything like that. Or would she?* Molly's thoughts fly all over the place.

She looks deep into her mom's eyes. "Is this true?" her voice shakes.

". . .I. . ." her mother can't speak, instead, she nods.

"Oh my. . ." Molly falls to her knees. Covering her mouth, trying to hold in the sobs. They demand to leave her body.

*How. . .how didn't I know? My mom, she. . . she does drugs. No. I can't, no. There's no way.* Molly denies every bit of it.

*It'd explain why she has been acting so weird.* Molly slowly admits to herself.

"Hunny. . .I'm sorry." Jen kneels down beside Molly.

She looks at her mother firmly in the eye.

"No more lies," she states bravely. "Are you seriously planning to spend the rest of your life with him?"

No more sugar coating. She wants to know what the future has planned.

"Yes." Jen says, easily. "Of course, he is my husband. It gets hard at times but that doesn't mean that you give up."

She drops farther to the ground, grabbing ahold of her throbbing throat. *No! No, please no. This can not go on forever.* Molly thinks between her sobs.

"We are planning on all of it. Love is hard, but you have to work for it. And I want to work through it with him, I love him. We will get a house, have more kids hopefully. . ." Jen's

~ *Riley Brett* ~

words turn to a blur, Molly can only hear the mumbled voices within the room.

Her body prickles with pain. It's simply inevitable.

There is nothing she can do.

No matter what she says.

It doesn't matter.

None of it matters.

Not a single thing.

Numbing tears slip down her damp face. Her red watery eyes look directly into Jen's, trying to find her mother. Trying to hold on tightly to who she once was. At least who Molly *thought* she was.

*She will never get it. She will never know how bad it hurts. She doesn't even want to know.* Molly thinks. *I wish she knew.*

. . .

Everything blurs past her. Going back to the apartment fights weekly, and bullies at school along with the kids around the apartment. Including the fight that led to Molly trying to call her grandparents. Her hands shook, trembling with sadness. As they answered, Noc ripped the phone from Molly's hand and smashed it against the wall. Shattering it to pieces. He looked her in the eye and aggressively told her not to call anyone ever again. Especialy her grandparents.

Everything until today. Today Molly wakes up feeling off, tired, and on edge.

Today is different. Even different than New years eve.

There isn't just tense air, there is fear. Everywhere.

Molly rolls out of bed, luckily it is a Saturday so she puts a movie into her DVD player planning her lazy day.

She opens her door, looking around the apartment. Trying to find something. She doesn't know what, but she knows there is something that needs to be found.

Nothing speaks out to her, so she proceeds back to her room and turns on the TV. She spends her lazy morning in her bed, with her door halfway open. Open enough to see down the hallway.

Throughout the morning Jen spends a while getting ready in the bathroom. Pacing between the bathroom and her bedroom. Robe wrapped tightly around her, and a towel holding up her wet hair.

Noc speaks to her as she walks between the two rooms, both talking casually.

Until Noc's voice rises.

Jen walks back to the bathroom. Noc sprints after her, clenching her neck into a chokehold. Ripping her down. . . dragging her by the neck into their room. Jen's eyes bulge at the suffocation and shock.

His arm flexes around her weak neck, gripping ahold of her tightly. Jen fights against it, grabbing onto his arm.

"Mom!" Molly screams. Shaking down deep inside her bones.

He throws her onto the bed and shuts the door, leaving it cracked slightly. Open enough for Molly to see her mother sobbing on the bed. Begging him to stop. Begging for mercy. Promising to do whatever he told her to do.

"Please. . . please, don't hurt me," Jen says softly, cries releasing from every part of her body.

*Mom! No please no. Don't hurt her.* Molly cries, standing beside her door in shock.

She can't call anyone because her phone is broken. *I can run to the neighbors.*

Molly shakes, wobbling at her knees.

*Please be ok. Please don't kill her.* Molly pleads in her thoughts. If only she could stand up to him and say the things she says in her mind.

She pushes her fear aside and runs through the apartment and unlocks the door. Hoping and praying she can get out quick enough. Every single blood cell shakes.

She manages to unlock all the locks and enters the hallway. *The landlord. He will help.* Molly thinks.

She sprints down the hall and reaches the door.

-knock, knock, knock-

She hits the door as hard as she can with the trembles weakening her arms.

Nobody answers. "C'mon. Please answer." Molly pleads.

She gives up on the one door and moves to the next.

-knock, knock, knock-

Still no answer.

She runs farther down the hallway and reaches another door.

-knock, knock, knock-

"Please answer," Molly whispers.

"Hold on." a lady calls out. She has an accent as if English isn't her first language.

"Yes!" Molly says under her breath. *Thank you.*

"Hello?" the lady opens the door.

"Hi. . . can I. . . call the-the police. . . please?" she stutters, all of the tears tightening her throat. She hopes the tears don't fully close her throat, she is already having trouble breathing as it is.

"Sure, yeah come in." the lady opens the door and waves Molly in.

Molly runs in, holding onto her tears as best as she can.

"Here sweetie. What is your name?"

A boy comes walking in from the other room.

"I'm, um Molly." she tries not to stutter this time, but her throat is closing tighter by the second.

Molly grabs the phone and dials with her shaking fingers. 9-1-1

The phone rings loudly in her ear.

"Nine-one-one, what is your emergency?" a woman answers.

". . ." Molly tries to speak but she gets choked up.

"Hello?" the woman speaks again.

"Hi, I. . . I, my mom she uh, she is hurt. My mom and her husband are fighting, please help." she finally finds her words. Not what she wanted to say but better than nothing.

"Ok sweaty, what is your address?"

"Oh, um. . . I don't know."

"Ok, that's alright we can run the address of the call."

The women ask more questions, about Molly's age and her mother's last name. Everything comes out shaky and stuttery.

"Alright, we have sent a few officers to you. They should be there shortly. Do you mind staying on the phone until the officers get there or do you feel ok going back and waiting?"

*Go back? Did she not hear the part about them fighting? Maybe I am just overreacting again and this is normal.* Molly thinks to herself.

"I'll stay on the phone."

"Ok, sweetie." the woman says and proceeds to make conversation.

Sirens come from outside and they end the call.

Molly hands the phone back to the lady in the apartment. "Thank you."

"Is everything alright?"

". . .Yeah." *That's why I called 9-1-1 because everything is alright.* Molly thinks.

"Will you be alright?"

"Yeah, thank you so much for letting me use your phone."

Molly looks back and forth between the women and her son, a twinge of jealousy flares in her chest, she wants that mother kid bond so badly.

"Ok, of course." the lady smiles, closing the door as Molly walks into the hall.

*No! This is not ok. This is not normal, I don't care what anyone says. This is far from normal.* Molly thinks angrily.

She makes her way down the hall and sits around the corner of their apartment door. Waiting for the officers to make their way inside.

She sits there alone. scared, and confused.

. . .

After a few minutes, the officers come and bring Molly back into the apartment. Jen looks Molly in the eye, stunned that she would call the police.

Like before, the police don't help and they leave within minutes of coming. Jen assures them it had just been an accidental call.

Molly's heartbreaks, more than slightly. And why should it come as a surprise to Molly? This outcome has already happened so many times already, it would be crazy to think there could ever possibly be a different one.

She grabs ahold of her waist and grips tightly. *This isn't love. At least I hope it isn't.* Molly thinks to herself. Sitting along her bedroom floor, holding onto her knees tightly. Her heart trembling with pain and in desperate need of help.

Cool tears drip slowly down her lost face. She breathes in deeply, coming more as a sniffle from her stuffed up button nose. The room fills with darkness, no light in sight.

She hangs her head. *This can not be what love really is. . . it just can't be.*

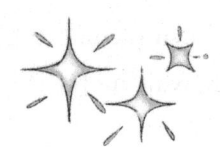

## Chapter 5

# Bravery

Molly grabs the microwave popcorn from off of the counter. Smelling all of the buttery goodness.

"Hurry up you're going to miss the beginning!" Jen says from the living room.

"I'm coming, I'm coming," Molly replies running to the couch.

It's girls night, Molly and her mother are watching a newly released movie and eating popcorn.

"Thank you," Jen smirks, grabbing the bowl from Molly's hands.

"Hey!" she giggles.

Jen throws a piece of popcorn in Molly's face.

Laughs fill the room as the movie starts.

After the cops had come, many fights broke loose over a few weeks. Some fights led to Jen and Molly hurrying to a hotel and staying the night.

Ever since that one day, she has been on edge. Paranoid about everything. She doesn't want that to happen to her mother again, though there isn't anything that she can do nor could have done. That simply breaks her heart.

For the first time in so long, Molly and her mother get a chance to have a girl's night. Just the two of them. Noc is out with his friends for the night, so they get the apartment all to themselves. She hasn't been this excited in so unbelievably long.

Even if it is only for a night, she will enjoy every second of it.

Throughout the evening they do many things; they laugh at ridiculous comments, paint each other's nails with crazy colors, gossip about the corny movie, and share popcorn from a huge bowl. It is amazing.

"If that happened to us, and we got separated. I would run into your arms and never let go." Jen says, referring to the movie." Not ever." she looks Molly deep in the eye.

Molly can feel the intensity of her mother's eyes. Knowing she is serious about every word she had just said.

"I wouldn't either," Molly replies softly, tears burn in her eyes.

-pound-

The door flies open.

Noc begins to yell, so loud Molly can't tell what he is saying.

"What? Calm down!" Jen yells, waving her hands down.

Noc shifts his jaw.

~ Riley Brett ~

*Oh, please no.* Molly thinks, remembering the signs he would give off when he was using before; The jaw shifting, leg twitching, erratic behavior, and constant yelling.

Noc runs over to Jen and pulls her into their bedroom, continuing to yell furiously.

Molly shifts her eyes to the big window, staring upon the beautiful sunset. She pulls herself to the window and watches the clouds move across the dim sky.

Her heart pounds with anxiety.

She breathes heavily.

*It's just another fight, it'll be ok. . .* Molly tries to convince herself.

-Inhale. . . exhale-

She slows her breathing.

Her cool hand glides along her frightened skin.

"It'll be ok," she whispers. Moving her hands along the windowsill, spreading her fingers across the cold surface.

Watching the sky, she feels her dreams form upon the sky, just as the sun goes down. Disappearing past the horizon.

She walks past the loneliness of the apartment and enters her room, puts a movie in, and feels the television give her comfort. As if she isn't fully alone.

. . .

"Molly. Molly get up, pack as many things as you can. We are going back to Caput." her mother says, pulling Molly's blanket down from her body.

Molly opens her eyes to the bright overhead light. "What?" she yawns.

"Don't ask I will explain later. Let's go, we have to be gone by the time he gets back from work." Jen replies, walking out of the room.

*Leaving? Why?* Molly wonders.

She drags herself out of bed and begins to gather as many things as she can.

Packing takes very little time for Molly, she is already so used to it.

She gets herself cereal for breakfast and watches people go about their morning from the big window aside from the kitchen table. Her head wobbles, she could have slept for a few more hours.

Last night was a long night, when she finally fell asleep, nightmares trapped her in a dreading place. It was so dark, so abandoned, and full of scary villains.

"When you are done packing your room, please start packing other things of ours around the apartment," Jen says, grabbing a cup of coffee.

"Ok." Molly manages to say.

She finishes her bowl of cereal and begins to pack, in a state of lassitude.

Yawns escape her body often, yet she continues to pack throughout the morning. Thinking about so many things, too many to keep track of.

~ *Riley Brett* ~

Everything she gets to go back to, all of her friends and family. She is so excited to see them all again. It has been horrifying to be away from everyone for so long.

Jen walks quickly between rooms in the apartment, gathering items of theirs and packing it into as few bags and boxes as possible.

"Hey mom, can I go play outside? I finished packing." Molly asks, walking into her mother's room.

"Yeah, that's fine. Be careful."

"Ok, thanks."

Molly already packed her snow gear, she leaves in her regular clothes.

The huge snow pile alongside the building is just waiting to be played in. She runs up the steep side, gripping onto ice chunks sticking out from the huge pile.

The pile is icy and hard to grip, her shoe loses friction and she slips down slightly. She pushes her boots into the snow, gaining a stable push.

Once she finally makes it to the top, she spreads her arms out and feels the cold wind blow along her face. Her breath releases into the air, creating a puff before her face.

"Hey Molly." a boy smirks. Standing a few feet in front of Molly.

*Shoot. Please not today.* Molly feels her throat tighten.

He comes closer, his smirk turning into an evil leer.

"What do you want?" Molly says, taking steps farther and farther back.

"Oh, won't you play with me?" he steps closer.

"No, not today. I am moving." she takes another step, her footsteps reach the mid-air.

She quickly wobbles forward, catching her breath. The edge to the tall snow pile lays inches away from her foot. "C'mon, move out of the way."

"Oh you mean this way." he steps to her left blocking her escape to the building.

*No...* She feels a piece of herself fade, a piece of bravery.

She bolts to the right trying to escape. Her boots dig into the loose snow with each step, slowing her down. Her legs fight on, burning and aching. Every inch of her body fights, every inch fights against the snow, the sadness, the fear. Everything.

Footsteps come closer and closer.

He tackles her and shoves her face-first into the snow.

"I can't breathe." Molly feels her breath sink into the air." Please. . ." she can't make out the rest of the words her throat is too tight.

Tears spill down her face and into the snow.

She fights for air, gulping and gasping

He tightens his grip around her kneck, shoving her freezing face deep into the snow.

His fingertips dig into her skin.

"I. . . I. . . can't breathe," Molly yells out one last time.

He gives no sign of releasing her.

Her hands fight through the snow. Gripping onto fluffy, fresh snow. Fighting harder and harder.

~ *Riley Brett* ~

*He doesn't get to bully me. Not today. I have to persevere.* Molly feels bravery spark within her.

-Inhale. . . exhale-

She musts up all of her strength and rolls over on her back. Looking into his face she feels anger flare.

He fights back.

*It hurts.* More tears slip as he grips along her kneck.

Her face is so cold, she is sure it will forever stay cold.

She pulls every last bit of strength and pushes him off.

He rolls aside, surprising Molly herself.

She runs as fast as she can to the left, heading for the building.

"Yeah you better run!" the boy yells after her.

She doesn't look back.

The apartment door opens and she runs inside. She collapses to the floor, gliding down the wall. Weezing, and trying to catch her breath.

She can still feel his hand around her kneck. Gripping her cold skin. She thought for sure she wouldn't make it out of his tightly clenched hands.

Tears race down her cheeks, freezing upon her cold skin.

She rubs her hand along her kneck, where his hands had been. Her kneck tender and cold.

Why does everyone pick on her so much? Is she just easy to make fun of? Or is it because she isn't who everyone else wants her to be?

She debates whether she should tell her mother or not. They're moving anyway, so what difference does it make?

As soon as she can refill her lungs with warm air, she climbs up the stairs and drags herself into the apartment.

She closes the door behind her and rests her hands on her knees.

"You ok?" Jen asks, walking into the living room.

Her throat tightens. "Yeah. . . no. . . I mean, a boy just bullied me." she says slowly as if she is trying to comprehend it herself.

"What? What did he do?"

"He tackled me, and. . . and shoved my face into the snow . . ." she doesn't mention the fact that he got on top of her and held her there by her kneck. Or the fact that she couldn't breathe.

"Oh Hunny, I'm sorry. We are moving, so you won't have to deal with him any longer." Jen smiles, and grabs another box to gather more items. "Why don't you get some food and rest a bit."

"Alright."

His hands. His cold hands against her warm kneck.

Luckily her hair is long enough to cover most of her keck, and her hood was up protecting her head from the snow. But that didn't stop it from covering her face and falling down her chest. And it sure didn't stop his tight grip against her fair skin. Digging and tearing, taking her breath. . . her voice.

The shiver sits shockingly under her skin and within her tight throat.

Tears have choked her up, delaying her words. She feels even more speechless than before. How could that be possible? She was already so voiceless. So vulnerable.

The only difference is the way she handled it. She thinks back to how she escaped his tight grip. *Bravery.*

She found her inner braveness, even in such a difficult moment.

She found a part of her voice, and she owned it.

She embraced the fear, and she persevered through it.

Even with the bravery, she feels weak. So weak, it is hard to move. Her hands shake rapidly. Her eyes tremble with painful tears.

*Stop. How do I stop shaking? Please make it stop. . .* Molly begs herself. Knowing there is nothing anyone can do at this point, the trauma has already ripped through a part of her memories.

A thought pops into her head, sparking ambition through her veins.

*Soccer. Soccer can make me feel better.* Molly thinks, widening her eyes at the thought. *But how will I play soccer in the snow, alone?*

The idea of playing aggressive, competitive soccer makes her smile ear to ear. Running as fast as she can up the field, the wind blowing against her sweaty skin. Breathing in the BO of other girls, gross, but familiar and oddly comforting. Most importantly, the feeling of the ball at her cleats, rolling along the dry grass. Her cleats making the most perfect sound as it pounds along the ball with every touch. It is the most magnificent sound to ever fill her ears.

The thought soon fades, realizing she won't be able to play until she is back in Caput anyway.

*Caput, I have to hurry up and pack before he gets home.* Molly thinks anxiously.

She hurries over to her mother, "Do you need help packing anything?" she asks.

"Uhm, no we are good for the most part. You could start bringing things out to the car." Jen says, putting clothes into a suitcase.

Molly gathers her bags first and brings them down to the truck. She keeps her eyes on the lookout for any kids, especially for the boy. Her heart races as she runs out to the truck. Quickly placing all of the items neatly into the back end.

More bags and boxes are gathered from the apartment. Jen places items by the door for Molly to bring down.

She works hard all evening, lifting heavy and lightboxes. The apartment looks so empty without their things lying around. It looks the exact way it did before she had come. Lonely and plain.

The sky begins to darken, making Molly's nerves spike like crazy. She wants to leave before he gets back from work. If he came back to see them leave, he would for sure kill one of them. If not one, both.

Boxes and bags fill the truck. Almost every inch is taken up. Garbage bags take up most of the space, filled with clothes and other miscellaneous things.

Molly gathers snacks from the apartment and stuffs it all into a lunch box. Preparing for the long car ride back to Caput. Oddly enough, she loves car rides. They bring a thrill in the comfort of your own car and blankets. She gets to snuggle up and watch movies on the screen attached to her seat. Jen had them put in recently, just after they got back from vacation.

The vacation was scheduled for quite some time, Molly, her grandparents, and her mother all went on an amazing vacation. It was a trip she will remember forever. She got to go on rides, get facepaint, eat ice cream, have fancy dinners, and so much more.

"Mom, do you need help with anything else?" Molly asks, walking over to her mother in the kitchen.

"No, I think we're good. Do you have everything you need?" Jen asks.

"I have everything in the car. Can we go?"

"Yeah, go ahead I will be down in a sec."

"Alright." Molly looks back at her mother and pleads "Please hurry."

Molly grabs her lunch box and proceeds to the truck.

Anxiety pulses through her veins. The thought of seeing him again truly sickens her.

She crawls into the backseat of the truck and makes a little nest. Combined of blankets and things to do for the car ride. She sets her lunch box right beside her water bottle.

Garbage bags surround her seat. They had to improvise, there was no time to go buy boxes and totes. Thank goodness garbage bags can hold so much, the box was empty by the time they had completely finished packing.

Minutes go by, slowly as if all the time in the world was passing at once. Molly feels her patience wane away. Jen has yet to come out.

*What if he comes? What will he do to us once he sees that we are trying to leave?* Molly thinks to herself. Being alone gives her thoughts time to form and question everything.

Her mind tenses by the second.

*I should run in and see if she is alright.* Molly thinks, pushing the car door open.

Before she can get out of the car, her mother comes walking out of the building.

Pressure releases from Molly's chest, freeing her from the pulsing worry and fear.

Jen puts a suitcase into the back end. She comes around to the driver's side and sets her purse down below the passenger seat; which is full of items. "Ready?" she asks.

"Yeah," Molly says eagerly.

*Come on let's go. We need to leave before he gets back.* Molly's worries abrupt her thoughts again.

A black sports car whips into the parking lot, causing snow to fly up beside its wheels.

*Is that? Is it him?* Molly wonders, her heart racing at the thought.

The car door opens, but before the face is revealed their truck speeds out of the parking lot.

*It was.* Molly confirms to herself.

*~ Riley Brett ~*

Their truck continues to roll down the road eventually reaching the highway.

Not many words are exchanged between Molly and her mother during this drive, but they do talk about school back in Caput and how that will work out.

They will be staying in a room back at Jen's old duplex until they can find a place of their own. For tonight they will stay at Jen's friend's house.

The road grows dark, Molly's eyes begin to tire and burn. But off in the distance, she can see bright shining lights, it's the city. They're almost there.

Her smile widens as her eyes close. She dozes off, hoping to clear her mind and prepare herself for whatever tomorrow may have in store for her.

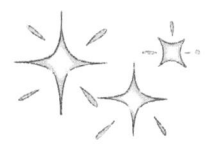

## Chapter 6

# The Power Of Invisibility

Freshly cut grass flies through the air as Molly's cleats rip through the dirt. Sprinting down the soccer field with the ball at her feet, nothing but opportunity and thrill ahead.

The field is wide open; it is only her and the goalie standing on the 6-yard box. Molly smirks, knowing it is a guaranteed goal. She fakes left then cuts right, towards the center of the field. She aligns her left foot inches from the ball and strikes it with her right foot, laces down. Black and white spiral through the air, spinning in the wind.

-swish-

The ball reaches the back of the net, just centimeters away from the crossbar.

~ Riley Brett ~

She runs to her team and cheers her way back to her starting position. The time is running low and the score is 2-1. Molly just put them in the lead.

A whistle blows and the ball glides along the grass, back to the opponent's feet. She sprints up the field, creating pressure amongst the attacking half.

The ball passes between the other team, Molly dives in aggressively. Creating a chance for the other team to mess up, pressure makes the opponent nervous. She pushes and maintains contact with one of the defenders, waiting to steal the ball.

"Molly go for it!" a teammate yells.

Molly doesn't hesitate, she flies in and jabs at the ball. She misses. The other team boots it up the field and tries to trap the ball beneath their feet. They fail, and the ball bounces towards Molly's team.

"Here, play it through," Molly yells.

Her teammate passes a quick hardball through, and Molly is off. She sprints towards the net, panting. Sweat drips down her rosy cheeks, droplets making their way into her eyes, blinding her of the field. She wipes her eyes with her jersey and continues up the field.

Footsteps get close, she can hear the speed in every step. All kinds of variables and plays crowd her mind, making it impossible to choose one. Instead, she freezes up, her legs ache from running for so long. She can't give up yet, she just can't.

Her calves throb and burn. Sweat drips down her arms.

She looks over to the sideline and sees her mother on her phone.

*What, she isn't watching?* Molly thinks, painfully.

Before she knows it the ball is at the opponent's feet. She lost the ball.

Every piece of pain in her body ignites, she feels the anger flare through her throbbing muscles.

*Not today. I get to win today.* Molly thinks competitively.

The defender runs up the sideline, not paying attention to Molly gaining momentum. Molly digs her cleats into the ground, gripping and ripping through the grass.

She bodies the girl and takes the ball. The girl flies off the field, and their whole bench gasps. But the referee doesn't call it, even surprising Molly.

She turns her body, opening herself to the field and finding all of her options. Only two defenders are in front of her. She has it from here.

Her feet tap along the ball, dribbling near the first defender, she reaches the girl and cuts to the left. Getting closer to the net, she spins around the last defender.

It is only Molly and the goalie now. She knows the goalie's skills at this point, she has tested multiple angles, figuring out their weaknesses and strengths.

She flexes her right leg and kicks as hard as she can into the net.

The goalie reaches for the ball, but it flies through her fingers and collides with the back of the net.

Her team cheers, along with the parents and coaches.

A whistle blows and they win 3-1.

"Good job Molly!" a teammate yells.

"Yeah, you too!" Molly yells back, walking over to her mother and father.

"Good job sweety!" Sam says, pulling Molly's sweaty body into a tight hug.

Little Sam comes running over with one of his plastic toys. "Good game Molly," he says, nudging her shoulder.

"Thanks, Sam" she giggles.

"Hey, we are going to go get some ice cream. Would you want to come with?" her father asks.

"She is going to her cousin's house in a little bit so it can't take too long." Jen cuts in.

"Alright, your call Molly."

"I want to, but I still have to pack."

"Ok, next time we can. That was a great game, I love watching you play." her father smiles.

"Thank you, and thank you for coming." Molly hugs him tightly.

He kisses her on the forehead and releases her. "We are going to head out then, I love you, and call me when you get the chance."

"I love you too, I will."

Her mother grabs her chair, "Ready to go home?" she asks.

"Yeah," Molly replies, chugging the rest of her water.

"Grandma Albany will be there shortly to pick you up. So you have to pack quickly, ok?"

"Ok."

...

Molly packs her bag as quickly as she can when she gets back. They are renting a house, just a few blocks away from their old one. Molly insisted that they move by T, now they are only two blocks apart.

A couple of months have gone by since they moved back. They have been staying at this new house for most of that time. It is a top and bottom duplex, they stay in the bottom half. It is a two-bedroom place, it is small but it does its job.

The soccer season just ended, the recreational team that she is on has been playing for a while now. Their team has yet to make it past the playoffs, but Molly did win a trophy this year. A shiny gold-colored trophy printed "U8 Caput Soccer"

Molly just turned 8 last month. She had a party in their backyard, the kids played for hours on the trampoline and had all kinds of snacks.

It is almost the 4th of July, Molly is spending it with her cousins out of town.

Not much has been said about Nocens, Molly is glad she doesn't have to hear his name. Though it is still a growing fear, he hasn't called or anything. From what she knows.

She is excited to go spend time with her cousins and Dollan. He has been living with her Aunt and Uncle for a while now. Molly has been able to visit a few times, but not as much as she would like. Her grandmother (Dollan's mom), brings Molly with whenever she goes. Especially during the summertime.

"Molly! Albeny is here." Jen yells through the house to Molly.

"Alright, I will be out in a second," Molly replies, grabbing her bag and blanket. She brings her blanket everywhere, it comforts her wherever she is.

She runs through the house and out through the door. "Hey grandma!" she says, smiling widely.

"Hey, Molly!" Albeny welcomes Molly with a great big hug. "I have missed you."

"I missed you too." she grips tighter.

"Are you ready to hit the road?" Albeny loosens her grip.

"Yep! Bye Mom, I love you." she gives Jen a quick hug, and runs to the car.

"I love you too, call me when you get there," Jen yells as Molly closes the car door.

She rolls down the window and blows her mother a kiss, "I will call you as soon as I get there." she yells out, while the car begins to roll along the road.

Jen blows a kiss back, Molly soon loses sight of her mother and settles back into her seat.

Molly can't wait to see her cousins, Aunt, and uncle. She hasn't seen them all in so long. Most of all she can't wait to see Dollan and play all kinds of fun games and to learn new magic tricks. Dollan has the best magic tricks, they are crazy good, it blows her mind.

Along the ride, she daydreams her typical dreams. Creating imaginative stories with the shapes of the clouds. These stories aren't just any story, they are ones created for her own future. Ones she wishes to come true.

She imagines people, conversations, and all kinds of other things. Fun things she can do with her cousins and her dad. It is a whole other kind of reality she puts herself in.

"How is soccer going?" Albeny asks.

"Good. We had our last game of the season today, we won 3-1." Molly replies. Leaving her imaginative reality.

"Oh wow, that's pretty cool. Did you score any goals?" Albeny asks, making eye contact with Molly through the rear-view mirror.

"Yeah, I scored 2. I would have gotten more." she shakes her head in disappointment. She could have done better, though she is her own toughest critic as her father(Sam) would say.

"Wow, 2 goals. That's pretty good, I wouldn't be so hard on yourself. It is good to reflect, but it is also good to pat yourself on the back." Albeny smiles in the mirror.

"Thank you." she thinks about that for a second. *If I am not hard on myself then who will be? I want to get better, even if that means being really hard on myself.*

"Did you eat before I picked you up?"

"No, I had just gotten back from my soccer game."

"Ok, would you like to stop and get some food?"

"Sure."

~ *Riley Brett* ~

The car ride is faster than normal. They go on to catch each other up on things that have been going on since they have seen each other last. On their way down the highway, they pick up food from a drive-through. Then continue along the road.

Molly pictures how she will greet everyone when she gets there. She misses her dad(Dollan) so much, she hasn't seen him in a long time.

She daydreams running into his arms and never letting go. Then playing with scooters and chalk in the driveway.

The sky darkens, and the clouds begin to fade. All that is left in the sky is a pink and orange sunset, slowly falling beneath the trees. She lets the view consume her eyes, enjoying the beauty and peace.

A deep breath keeps her concentration deep within the sky. Feeling every effect of the skies glory. It is a site ever so rare, and peaceful. She lives in every second of it.

Until it fades into the distance, for others to watch and enjoy.

A smile fills her face. Making her cheeks grow pink.

Trees soon crowd her view of the darkened sky.

They pull into a driveway.

"We're here!" Molly yells, jumping out of the car. Gathering her bag and blanket.

Albeny giggles at Molly's excitement. "Hold on now dear, we have a few things to grab." she says, grabbing bags from the back end.

"Oh right." she giggles.

They gather bags and other items.

"Molly!" her cousins come running out.

"Hey!" Molly hugs both of them.

Molly has three cousins; Gloria, the oldest and plays all kinds of sports, Lae, who is 3 months older than Molly, and they do everything together, and Cora, who is the newest addition to the family.

"Wait where is my dad?" Molly asks.

"Oh, I forgot to tell you, Molly. He won't be here for this visit." Albeny answers before her cousins get the chance.

"What? Why not?" she gets teary-eyed.

"Uhm, he is in Jail for a few days."

"For what?"

A few seconds go by before anyone answers her.

"Drinking and driving," Gloria responds.

Molly pauses for a second.

Memories flood her mind. . .

*In the bowling alley parking lot, Dollan and Molly sitting on a curb waiting for her mother to come out.*

*Little leaves blow within the air, floating slowly as if they never want to land.*

*Others come spiraling by, twisting and spinning until they fall upon the ground.*

*"Hey want to see something?" Dollan asks.*

*"Sure." Molly smiles.*

*Dollan picks up a leaf, "It is called a helicopter leaf." he lifts it up for Molly to see. "It is called that because when you throw it up into the air it falls down, spinning like a helicopter."*

*Molly smiles with excitement.*

*Dollan jumps up and releases one into the air. It flies away from them, spinning and spinning.*

*She smiles in awe. "Can I try it?"*

*"Of course. Here." he hands her a leaf.*

*Molly brushes her fingers along the thin part of the leaf. Studying its features and what makes it so unique.*

*She jumps as high as she can, and let's go.*

*It flies quickly from the jumping point down to the ground's surface.*

*"Wow," she whispers. Something so simple yet so cool.*

*She gathers more and more. Running around the parking lot. They see who can grab the most.*

*Before they know it. Multiple little leaves are spiraling through the breeze. Crowding the air, they fall upon the ground clashing with one another.*

*"I can put you on my shoulders and you can let them go from higher up," Dollan says, picking up as many helicopters as he can.*

*"Ok!" she grabs a few more, trying to find ones that are perfectly whole.*

*He gathers the leaves and sets them down. "Here, you can hop onto my shoulders."*

*"Ok." she climbs onto his back and onto his shoulders.*

*To her, she is so high up in the air she can see more than she could before. She can see the lake spreading for miles down the street, the water glimmering from the sun rays. It's beautiful.*

*"Here you go," Dollan says, handing her the helicopters.*

"Thanks." she carefully gathers them into her hands.

Inspecting them to make sure they are ready for flight.

She grabs one at a time and cautiously drops it into the air. Letting it glide through the breeze, she watches the leaf fall ever so freely. She wonders what it would be like as that leaf. Letting herself relax upon the breeze. Feeling every oxygen molecule blow along with the thin floating leaf.

How peaceful it must be to spiral in the wind all day.

She is down to 5 leaves. Instead of throwing them individually, she puts them into one hand and throws them up.

They spread apart from one another as if they had opposite attractions.

Each leaf flows along a different path, most likely because each one had little defects along their thin surface causing their flight to fly away from one another.

She watches as each leaf hits the ground at a different time, colliding with the hot tar.

She spreads her arms as if she was a free-falling leaf. And enjoys the breeze, blowing along her fair cool skin. Breathing in the fresh air.

"That's what I am talking about," Dollan says happily.

Molly giggles at her dad's dorkiness.

. . .

The memory fades as she remembers how much time has changed.

"Oh." she stutters.

"Yeah, but we will still have fun. Don't worry." Albeny says, carrying things into the house through the garage door.

The house is beautiful. It is a two-level home with 3 bedrooms, a big backyard with a swing set, and a nice open living room.

Molly loves it here. It is her other home away from home.

The three of them play video games, draw with chalk, play on the swingset, and all kinds of other games. Apart from all of the fun, their house is comforting and safe.

"Let's go play hide and go seek," Lae suggests, running back into the house.

Gloria follows close behind her.

Molly stands for a moment, in the dark quiet driveway. Taking in the fact that her dad won't be here, at all. Tears form in her eyes, but she pushes them away.

*When did I get so emotional?* She wonders.

She forgets about it and runs inside.

Through the door, she enters into a shoe area and takes off her slides.

"Hey, Molly. Good to see you." Molly's uncle greets her with a hug.

"Hi, good to see you too." her face squishes into his arms.

"Hey Molly." her aunt comes walking over with their new baby, Cora. "Do you want to hold her?"

"Of course!" Molly opens her arms, pulling the baby in." She is so pretty." she says in awe.

A beautiful girl with big brown eyes. Molly wonders what it will be like when the baby grows older and can play with the rest of them.

~ *Passion From Within* ~

*I wonder what is going on in her little mind?* Molly thinks, looking into her big eyes.

"She is adorable," she says.

"Isn't she?" Molly's aunt replies.

Molly hands Cora back to her Aunt.

The baby is so precious.

So innocent.

Molly can't wait to see how she grows up.

"Molly c'mon," Gloria yells from their bedroom.

She runs into their bedroom, on the second floor. Their room has two beds and a tv, it is the perfect size for both Gloria and Lae.

"We are going to play hide-and-seek, ok?" Lae says.

"Alright, who counts first," Molly asks.

"One, two, three-nose goes," Gloria yells out, touching her nose and dropping quicker than Molly can focus.

Before she knows it they are both already touching their nose and dropped to the floor.

"Dang it. I'm always it."

"Yeah because you're slow." Gloria giggles.

Molly teases back, mocking her facial expression.

Molly and her cousins tease each other as if they were all siblings. It comforts Molly to know she has her own sibling on Dollan's side of the family, Cassity. Cassity was born when Molly was six, meaning that Cassity is now 2, but Molly hasn't gotten to spend much time with her. She wants to know her sister more, she wants to have a bond with her just like the bond

Gloria and Lae have. Though it's hard when she can't even see her Dollan.

"Fine. Go hide."

Both of the girls laugh and run out of the room.

Molly covers her eyes and counts to 30. "1, 2, 3–" she doesn't make it to 4 before she hears her cousins creep down the stairs." Ha, I know exactly where they are going," she whispers to herself.

There is a dark laundry room in the basement where they always hide, though most of the time they are too scared to hide in there alone. So instead they hide together. Other than that there isn't anywhere else in the basement to hide.

"29, 30-ready or not here I come," Molly yells, not too loud because she doesn't want them to hear that she is done counting yet.

She tiptoes out of the room and down the stairs. The basement is finished with carpet and everything, but when it is dark, it is very scary. There are very few windows down there, which means when there are no lights on it is mostly pitch black.

"Serious, you guys had to hide down here," she whispers while walking cautiously down the dark stairway.

The stairway splits off in two directions, left and right. To the left there is a room, that is their great grandfather's room, nobody goes in there. And to the right is a huge open spaced living room with a tv, couch, and an indoor hockey net. Across from the hockey net, there is a door, a door that leads into the dark big laundry room.

She scans the basement, trying to see if they are anywhere but in that room." I am not going in there." she says under her breath.

*But I have to.* She reminds herself.

She shifts her feet along the carpeted floor and slowly over to the door. Her hand reaches the doorknob, slowly twisting it.

Her heart racing with fear. She doesn't do too well in the dark.

Her shaky hand pushes the door open. Across the room, a washer and dryer sit beneath a slim window. The rest of the room covered in cloths here and there.

Her heart still pounding against her chest, feeling it pulse in her wrist.

A sound comes from upstairs, she jumps in the suspense.

She takes deep breaths, trying to calm herself from the intense fear. Nobody is in the room. They must have hidden upstairs.

The basement still creeps her out so she runs out of the room. -ah!-

Her cousins pop out from behind the couch.

She jumps back, tumbling onto the floor. Grabbing onto her chest, "I thought you guys were in the laundry room." she says.

"Nope. Got you!" Gloria laughs.

"I guess you did. Another round before dinner?"

"Obviously."

The three of them play games all night until they all grow so tired they can't even speak correctly.

...

The smell of freshly cooked pancakes fills the air. Molly looks around the room, everyone is still sleeping. She gets out of bed and follows the delicious smell.

Grandma Albeny is cooking a big breakfast, early as usual.

"It smells amazing," Molly says, walking over to her grandmother.

"Thank you, good morning to you," Albeny replies, smiling back at Molly.

She rubs her eyes, trying to wake herself from the long night's rest. More nightmares had disturbed her sleep, just like every other night. This time it was even scarier because she wasn't in her own bed nor house though her cousin's house is very comforting.

She woke up in the middle of the night, just staring at the wall, trying to calm herself. The fear that reaches her in her dreams is far scarier than anything that has ever happened to her when she is awake. When she is in the nightmare, it traps her in this frightening reality. Even if she recognizes that it is just a dream, it consumes her and controls her by fear.

The dreams have gotten to be normal at this point. Though it isn't the fear itself that is normal, it is the regular assurance that doesn't surprise her in the slightest.

The fear that the dreams bring is beyond words. She is scared out of her skin in every dream, it isn't just monsters and zombies. It is real-life things that have happened or she has a fear of happening. Which makes it terribly worse.

*~ Passion From Within ~*

"Would you like some pancakes?" Albeny asks, interrupting Molly's deep thoughts. Molly is more thankful than anything at this moment.

"Yes, please. Thank you, grandma," she says, smiling towards her grandmother.

"Of course. Here is some syrup and berries." she sets them on the table.

Molly digs into the pancakes as soon as she gets them. Her mouth fills with wonderful flavor. "Oh my goodness these are amazing." she says with her mouth stuffed.

"Nothing too special." Albeny giggles.

Lae comes walking out of her bedroom, rubbing her tired face. "Do I smell pancakes?" she asks.

"Yes you do, come sit down and eat." Albeny dishes up some pancakes and fruit.

"Mmm, thank you." Lae sits down across from Molly.

Molly is still shoveling food into her mouth.

Lae tilts her head in confusion.

"Here you go." Albeny sets a plate in front of Lae.

"Thanks, grandma."

"Hey, we should go play on the playground when we are done eating," Molly says.

"Yeah."

"We can make mud cakes." Lae giggles.

Molly finishes her breakfast quickly and rushes to get ready. They both run out back at the same time, opening the sliding porch doors. In the backyard, there is a tree swing hanging next to the playground.

Molly runs to the tree swing, "Dibs on swinging first!" she yells out.

Her body flops onto the swing and flies back as she picks her feet up.

Cool summer air spreads across her face, filling deep into her lungs. The sky is grey and cloudy as if it will rain at any moment to come.

"Ok but I get to swing too," Lae replies.

Molly nods, enjoying the way her body swings freely.

"Hey." Gloria comes running into the backyard.

"Morning," Molly replies, gripping her feet against the ground to get more momentum.

"Can I swing too?"

"I called second," Lae says.

"Not if I get there first."

"What? No, I called dibs."

"So?"

Molly watches her cousins argue over who gets dibs. She wants that. Oddly enough, she wishes she could be their sibling instead of just a cousin. It seems comforting to have someone by your side to go through everything with. Sometimes she wonders what life would be like if she was closer to Cassity, and what things would be like if they lived together.

"Here one of you can have it," she says.

They both sprint to the swing, Gloria makes it there first.

*~ Passion From Within ~*

"Hey, I called dibs!" Lae yells out.

Instead of sitting there and waiting, she goes over to the playground itself and sits on one of those swings.

Molly walks over and sits down next to Lae.

"We can still make mud-cakes," Molly says.

"Ok."

Nobody moves for a little while. Everyone just enjoys the outdoor cool breeze.

"Hey, Molly! Someone is on the phone to talk to you." Molly's aunt yells out from the house door.

"Ok."

*Who could it be? Is it Dollan?* Molly wonders.

She runs up to the house and grabs the phone." Hello?" she says to the unknown caller.

"Hey, sweetie. Are you having fun?"

It's Jen.

"Hey Mom, yeah a lot of fun. What's up?"

"I just wanted to call and check on you. Also, I have somebody here who would like to talk to you." Jen says excitedly.

*Who could that be? The only person I want to talk to is Dollan and he is in Jail.* Molly's thoughts wander as the phone grows quiet.

"Hey Moll.–" a deep voice rattles through the phone.

*No. It couldn't be.* Her heart drops. *Could it?*

"How have you been? Your mother and I have missed you." the voice continues.

Her body shifts into a deafening silence.

Trembles create a chill along her skin. Her heart aches physically, pulsing against needling pain.

*No. He-they-she-, what is going on?* Molly's thoughts cut each other off as tears threaten her eyes.

"H-hi." she stutters.

"Did you have a fun fourth of July?"

"Y-yeah." her voice can't fight off the trembles within each breath.

"That's good. Alright, I am going to give the phone back to your mom ok? Love you." Nocens says, leading into a silence.

She is in so much pain she can't even cry. The tears won't come out, they are heald within her. Somewhere she can not reach, as if the tears are held captive in a dungeon in an unreachable place of her body.

*She. . . did they? Did they get back together?* All of her thoughts collide with one another in confusion and curiosity.

"Hey, sweetie. Doesn't he sound good? He got in an accident recently and was in the hospital for a little while. But he recovered and is getting better and better every day. His talking is getting better and his hearing, the injuries were really bad." her mother goes on.

Only one question layers her mind.

"Oh. . . so are you guys back together?"

"That's what I wanted to call and talk to you about. We thought we would give it another chance, the injury really scared me and made me realize I want to try things again. You and I will be moving back in with him as soon as you get back.

Isn't that great?" Jen's cheerfulness leaps through the phone. Making Molly feel sick.

"What? We are going back?"

"Try to be happy Hunny, this will be great."

*You said that last time.* Molly thinks, her guts churning.

"I already packed mostly everything up, we just have a few boxes left to grab when you get back."

"Oh."

"Anyway, I am glad to hear that you are having fun. Call me again later if you want, alright?"

"Ok."

"Love you to the moon and back, bye."

"Love you too."

The call ends.

Two teardrops slip down her cheeks.

"How could she go back to him? After everything," she whispers to herself. Wishing her dad was here to comfort her.

"Is everything ok?" Molly's aunt asks.

"Yeah. . . everything's fine." she quickly wipes her tears

Why does Molly do that? Why doesn't she tell people what is really going on and how she feels? Maybe it isn't everyone else who mutes her, maybe she mutes herself. But why? Why would she go out of her way to not speak? Or more importantly, what makes her feel like she can't tell anyone?

Everything feels numb. Emotionless and empty. As if her body has wholes taking away everything she consists of. As if her surroundings have disappeared, and the only thing around her empty body is the cool breeze. Blowing against her fragile skin.

She feels so meaningless.

So voiceless.

The one person she cares about most doesn't care to hear her voice. No matter what Molly says, that one person will never hear the pain within Molly's voice when she is screaming for mercy.

Mental pain goes unseen, yet causes the most damage. When others can't see things they choose to forget about it. What if the pain was no longer invisible? What if mental pain was able to be seen? Everyone would be able to see the scars that layer vulnerable bodies. Those who have been verbally abused, or have been through traumatic events.

When the pain goes unseen, it is easy to pretend it isn't there. Impressions come from the first sight of somebody, though the most important thing about a person is their inner purity. And what characteristics they possess, not what top they choose to put on in the morning.

*Your inner outfit.*

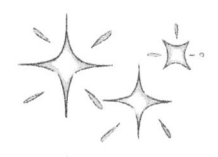

# Chapter 7

# Suffocation

Time gathers into a second, flashing in front of her eyes all in a moment. After the phone call, Molly shut down. She felt herself turn into an autopilot mode, where she didn't feel any emotions. Her confusion completely blinded her and made her happy moments pass too fast.

The move back to Metus takes no more than a week. Packing sure seems to be getting easy. All the practice seems to be paying off.

Molly says her goodbyes to T again, this time it is harder. She has no idea what will happen while she is gone, and leaving T means leaving part of her protection. Whenever T is around nothing seems to go wrong, and when things do go wrong, at least T is by her side.

~ *Riley Brett* ~

She grips her side tightly as she says goodbye. Walking back to her mother's car, they get on the road for the 4-hour drive awaiting.

Molly presses her head against her window, waving bye to her best friend. Until the truck turns the corner and she loses sight of T, *again.*

A deep breath cools her lungs.

Noc and Jen drove down together to meet Molly when she got back from her cousin's house. They packed up leftover boxes across the living room and left the keys.

The place was so empty, it was hard to look at. They just moved back, and they are already leaving again.

Thoughts fill her mind along the car ride. Whenever worries appear she tries to soothe her mind by figuring out how to solve those worries. Incase her worries were to happen she will be prepared.

She also watches movies on her tablet, laughing at animated characters across the screen.

The car ride seems to go by oddly quickly. She can't tell if it is because Noc drives faster than her mother or because she is lost in her tablet screen. Either way, they pull into the parking lot and park the truck.

Her heart drops.

All of the memories and anxiety floods back.

*Maybe this time it will be different.* Molly tries to convince herself.

Her eyes shift to the side of the building. Memories flash through her mind. . .

His cold hands. Her freezing face. Her lungs were desperate for warm air. The fight she fought, how her legs had ached and burned.

Tears burn her big hazel eyes.

She rubs her eyes quickly and opens her car door. Entering yet another reality, another chapter.

"Molly come help bring in the boxes, then we will go for a walk since it is so nice out," her mother says smiling.

"Ok," Molly replies, trying not to be rude.

Even though she can't stand the fact that they are back here, she wants her mother to be happy. She just hopes this will make her mother as happy as she thinks it will.

She gathers her bag and a few boxes. Following both Jen and Nocens into the apartment.

Anxiety and fear rush back into every blood vessel in her body.

The sight of her mother being pulled by her kneck flashes back.

The smell of the dinner Jen had cooked for Nocens, and he how pushed it away saying it wasn't good enough.

The phone being slammed against the wall and shattering to pieces.

Everything. Down to the last late-night cry.

Her body trembles in every emotion; anger, sadness, stress, anxiety, all except for happiness.

Late girl's night with her mom saved her from the daily dreadful events, but those only lasted for so long.

"Thanks, Moll. Now go unpack your room." Noc says, looking her firmly in the face.

She doesn't reply, only walks down the hall and into *her* room. The room is dim and empty, just as she left it. Taking a deep breath, she sets her bag on the ground and tries to relax.

For a little while, she imagines standing up to Noc, and telling him how well he should be treating her mother. How she deserves the world and she shouldn't receive anything less than that. Minutes turn into an hour, of her laying on her top bunk rehearsing how it will go, during the right moment.

*Only if I was brave enough to actually say any of this.* Molly snaps herself back into reality.

"C'mon Molly, we are going for a walk," her mother says, opening Molly's door.

She takes her focus off of the ceiling, "Ok, I'm coming." she replies.

-Inhale. . . exhale-

*It will be fine. Just try to keep things peaceful for as long as possible.* She prepares herself for as many possibilities as she can.

Molly walks into the room, seeing Nocens standing by the door, ready to venture out onto the streets of Metus. Jen standing anxiously, Molly can tell how bad her mother wants this to work.

*He better not hurt her again. She doesn't deserve to be hurt like that, nobody does.* Molly thinks firmly.

"Alright, let's go," Jen says, leading everyone out of the door.

The three of them walk down a lonely road. Very few cars pass them while walking to the park.

Molly walks ahead of Nocens and Jen. Being the first to explore what lays ahead, when she lived here last they didn't go to the park, mostly because it was winter and there was snow up to Molly's hips.

"Don't go too far ahead, Molly," Jen yells up to Molly.

"Ok," Molly replies, looking back and seeing the two of them hand in hand.

She lets out a sigh.

As much as she tries not to be mad about it, it still causes her a great amount of pain and anger. The way the two of them can just act as if nothing has happened. As if Noc hasn't grabbed Jen by her kneck, threatened her life, and so much more.

It must be different for Molly. The way that it is pressed permanently into her mind keeps her from ever forgetting about it, especially moving on from it. The memories bring her so much sadness and disparity.

She desperately hopes to grow past the pain it brings. And become stronger, it is a constant goal of hers.

A sound ruffles in the woods. Her heart rattles. She steps closer, trying to see what it could be, or who it could be.

Leaves sway.

Branches crunch.

Furr flies by in a blur.

Walking closer, she tries to see what is making so much noise. A bunny jumps out. Her chest collapses in relief. It is only a critter.

"Molly, where are you going?" Jen asks, from the side of the road.

"I heard something in the woods. It's just a bunny," she replies.

"Alright, come back here."

Molly watches the bunny, the way it stares cautiously at her. As if she will harm it. Its ears prop up, twitching at noises coming from around it.

*Why is it so suspicious of me?* She wonders.

The mammal's instinct kicks in, and it runs off. She tilts her head in confusion. Why did it run from her when she hadn't even done anything to it? Was it running because it was scared or had something hurt it and it is now on high alert?

Molly feels familiarity prick along her skin. It ran from her because it was scared it would be harmed, whether it was instinct or from experience, she feels the same way. The way she fears Noc, what he can do because of what he has done. It is her instinct, her way of protecting herself from what her brain detects as dangerous and harmful.

Voices rise from behind her. Noc and Jen are fighting.

*Here we go again.* She thinks, unsurprised.

"Well, what do you want me to do?" her mother raises her voice.

Noc tries to calm himself, in an effort to not scream and drag her by her hair." Stop making a scene Jen." he says, calm yet threatening.

"Or what?" she raises her voice again.

"I will call the police on you."

"Oh really? You would never do that, I have too much on you," she says snottily.

"You've been here not even a day, and we're already fighting." "Noc clenches his jaw." Cut. It. Out." his voice gets deep and tense. Rattling Molly's skin.

Crazy how his voice can have so much power, yet Molly can't even find her own voice.

Jen shrinks into her shoulders.

"You know you're a real piece of work," he mutters.

Jen's body becomes weak and layered in pain-filled vulnerability. Molly watches as her mother sinks into a different part of herself. *This isn't the happiness I was hoping for.* She feels her hope sink as her thoughts bring her mind back to reality.

Molly feels her own chest cave in. Seeing her mother like this, so hurt and quiet kills her, it absolutely kills her. She knows there is nothing that she can do to make it better, though she tries anyway. This is her chance to stand up to him and tell him how mean he is, how someone like him could never deserve a woman like her mother. She saves the heart filled speech for the perfect moment.

When they get back to the apartment, the fighting has calmed down, now it is only hurt feelings, and everyone walking around traps trying not to set off another fight. Knowing it would be much worse than the verbal fight outside.

"Hey, Noc can I talk to you about something?" Molly asks. Her hands sweating and her heart pounding.

"Yeah, sure Moll," Noc says, walking into her bedroom and sitting on the bottom bunk.

Her knees feel wobbly and unstable. She gets irritated with her body's reaction, and pushes everything aside. "You have been very rude to my mother, and she does not deserve it. She is a strong, brave, and beautiful woman. I think you need to respect her more." she says, coming out much more brave than she had thought it would.

"I agree, your mother is very beautiful. But she does know how to push my buttons, I will try to handle it better. That was just an argument outside, we are fine don't worry." Noc replies, calmly.

It went so much better than she expected, though she can't tell whether to believe him or not. His response was reassuring, but she still has so many walls of protection that it is hard to take him seriously.

"Ok, thank you." she manages to say, though she doesn't know if what he says is true she appreciates him not blowing a fume.

"Is that all?"

Oh, there is so much more, so many things she would love to say and get off of her chest. Telling him to leave us alone and never come back, he doesn't deserve the things he gets, he can't just beat upon her mother's body when he feels like it, he shouldn't scream at Jen the way he does, he could have and be so much more if only he realized how much pain he causes everyone. But most of all, there is more to life than hurting people, including self-harm. . .

"Yeah, that's all."

Jen stands in the doorway, smiling at Molly.

She smiles back at her mother, trying to comfort her mother's frightened mind.

Noc leaves the room, along with Jen, closing Molly's door behind them.

The room darkens as the sky grows pink. The sun is setting along the horizon, creating a breathtaking view.

She walks over to her window and rests her head along with her hand. Sighing at the day's challenges. Thoughts appear as she stares deep into the sky, dreaming as if she was asleep.

. . .

A couple of weeks fade by. Consisting of frozen yogurt on hot days and playing in the back parking lot for hours at a time. Fights breaking loose here and there, more verbal than physical. Although physical fights are scary and heart shaking, verbal fights are almost worse. You can say whatever you want, threaten whoever and whatever. The constant fear of it happening or not happening sitting along your skin makes an almost permanent itch. She covers her ears most nights or sleeps with her tv on.

At night is when she really comes alive, she doesn't have as many restrictions because nobody is around. She isn't allowed to leave her bedroom at night, not even to go to the bathroom. So basically imprisons herself in her room, where she has hidden snacks from the kitchen, not any liquids because she doesn't want to get yelled at for having to use the bathroom. She has prepared all of her art supplies, for the creative hours of the night just waiting to be tested and built. A corner in her closet is set up with piles of art supplies and things she had gathered throughout the day, preparing for the night.

During the winter months she had stayed here, she would lay awake for hours just watching the snowfall. Seeing the street lights magnify the shimmer along with each flake. The peacefulness that filled the outside air, soothed her body and her mind. Freeing her from anything and everything that brought her pain.

Today feels just like any other day. Except it is a Sunday, which means they are going out to eat because Noc is off of work.

Molly gets herself ready as if it is any other day, except today she is more antsy than normal. More eager to get out and explore what she hasn't already seen. It doesn't help much that it is a slow morning for everyone else. She is learning to not depend so much on others, mostly because she is always the first one ready for plans she hasn't even made. Being her mother who made the plans it is different, she respects that and continues to be the first one ready. With complaints here and there, that are sure annoying to those who are trying to get ready for the day.

After a morning of complaining, they make it out the door and into Noc's truck. The tension becomes tenser and tenser between Jen and Nocens. She ignores it, knowing it is usual for them to have tension.

Noc has a two-door pick-up truck, with three seats. Molly has to sit between the two of them.

She watches out the front window for new things along streets she hasn't seen. The scenery is full of trees and buildings. Until suddenly they pull in front of an apartment building, one different from theirs, rough and worn down. Green grass fills the front, along with bushy trees. Making her wonder what they are doing here.

"We are only stopping for a quick minute or two," Jen says, smiling over her shoulder as Noc jumps out.

"Ok," she answers, not questioning it much.

Her eyes scan the surroundings, the rest of the neighborhood is quite pretty. Nicely placed housing, evenly down the long road. All except for the apartment building, the old worn down building. So oddly placed, in the middle of a well-maintained neighborhood.

Her head tilts in confusion, "Why are we here?" she asks.

Jen hesitates, "Noc needed to visit a friend of his." she says.

Molly raises her left eyebrow. Even if he wasn't meeting up with a friend, what would she do about it?

Noc comes jogging back to the truck, opening Jen's door and handing her an item. Molly can't see what it is.

They leave the odd neighborhood, and head to eat somewhere.

Voices raise over Molly's head. Jen pulls the glove box open and handles a bottle of pills. Rattling while the truck rolls over bumps in the road. Jen pops the bottle open quickly and pops a pill into her mouth.

"No! Are you crazy? You can't have one of those, you will die." Noc raises his voice, slapping the bottle out of her hand.

"Too late." Jen raises her hands, fingers spread. She gulps, swallowing the pill.

"Throw it up! C'mon! I am getting you water so you will throw it up."

Noc speeds the truck up, racing between traffic.

They both scream back and forth over Molly's head.

*She will die?* Molly thinks, her heart drops into her stomach, boiling with fear and sadness.

"You are crazy! You can not have a full one! You knew that." his voice gets aggressive and irritated.

They swerve into a drive-through.

"Yeah, can I get a thing of water?" Noc says, "Ok, yeah."

The car pulls forward.

*She will die.* Her mind races again. Her chest pounds with anxiousness.

Noc pulls forward quickly. "Thanks."

He pulls out of the parking lot. Tires screeching.

"Drink the damn water. Throw it up! Now Jen." Noc's eyes bulge with anger.

"No!" her mother replies." Stop the car!" she insists.

Jen opens her car door, while the truck races down the street.

"Mom no!" she screams, grabbing at her mother." Please don't" she whispers.

~ *Passion From Within* ~

Tears begin to drip down her pale face. She feels so sick it hurts.

Jen glances at Molly, then looks back at Noc sternly. "Stop the car. I will jump out. Don't think I won't." she threatens.

"Jen don't be crazy."

"Stop the car!" Jen yells, rattling Molly's ear.

Within a second, Nocens grabs onto Molly's kneck. Gripping along her young, innocent skin.

*I can't. . . I can't bre-* Molly can't even finish thinking about her need for air.

His bicep flexes along her skin, cutting off her oxygen.

She grabs onto his arm, fighting and ripping.

Her eyes bulge in shock.

He pulls her in tighter as Jen doesn't close the door.

Molly fights, and fights. Trying to get even a molecule of oxygen.

Her nails grip into his arm.

"C'mon Jen, you know I don't want to do this." Noc almost pleads.

The truck drives unstably down the road.

Molly feels her eye site blur and goes slightly black.

"Mom. . ." her voice manages to plead, raspy and weak.

His grip loosens slightly. Just enough to gasp for air, gulping in as much as she can. Panting heavily, she feels her vision replenish.

Jen looks into Molly's eyes, and closes the door. "Let go of her." she yells.

"Throw it up," Noc says aggressively between his teeth.

His grip almost fully loosens.

She pushes his arm off of her, and curls into her seat. Out of instinct, she wants to go to her mother, but after that, she doesn't know who to turn to.

Her body shakes in shock. Her kneck is weak and throbbing.

The truck pulls into their apartment parking lot. "Get out." Nocens looks over at both of them.

Molly and her mother crawl out.

Noc speeds off.

She picks her hand up slowly, gliding her fingers along her red irritated kneck.

*He touched me. He actually took my breath from me. He-* Molly folds in pain and fear before she can finish the thought.

"C'mon, we have to go inside," Jen says, annoyed.

Molly follows her mother.

Jen stops in front of the apartment building door," He has my keys." her face fills with more anger. "C'mon." she looks down near Molly, not making eye contact.

Molly starts to follow her mother, a glimmer catches her eyes. She looks over at the glass and sees her reflection. Her kneck. . . it's red, there is a red mark around her kneck. Where his arm had been, where he took her breath. He physically took her breath, leaving her helpless and afraid.

*Why didn't I take my life when I had the chance.* Molly thinks back to her grandparent's home. The knife she had in her hand, even though it wasn't sharp enough to take her life. This time she wouldn't make the same mistake.

"Molly c'mon." her mother yells from the side of the building.

Molly looks at her reflection one last time. Wishing for it all to just end.

She runs alongside the building and to her mother's side.

"I have another set of keys in my truck," Jen says.

Tires screech around the corner. A truck pulls up beside them, rolling down the driver's side window.

"This is what happens to you, Jen," Noc yells. "When you decide to go against what I tell you. You should have just listened," he says with a smile, pulling down his dark shades.

Jen yells at the top of her lungs. Something about calling the police. Everything becomes a blur, all she can think about is the way he had taken her breath. How his arm was wrapped around her kneck, preventing any air to enter her body.

The tires spin, rolling the truck away quickly. Leaving black tire marks along the pavement.

Jen says something, but Molly doesn't comprehend a single word that is said.

Jen pulls Molly's arm with her as she storms across the parking lot. Dragging Molly's numb body.

Her kneck still throbs. Molly wonders if it will feel like this forever. If his arm will forever be imprinted on her kneck. Maybe the world will believe her, maybe people will finally understand what is going on. Suddenly she can not wait to tell the police.

"Are you going to call the cops?" Molly asks.

"Yeah, he took the truck and left us with no keys to get inside," Jen says, tapping against her phone's screen as if not having her keys is the only problem right now.

She won't have to say anything, they will just see it and know something is wrong. Hope flares across her trembling skin, finally, someone will do something. Someone will help her and her mother.

After a while of waiting, police sirens sound down the street.

*They're here.* Molly thinks happily.

Two cop cars pull into the parking lot.

The officers walk over to Molly and Jen. "Hello ladies, what seems to be the problem," he asks.

"Well, my husband took my truck and keys. We can't get into our apartment–." Jen continues, but Molly focuses on what she will say to the officer.

Finally, a silent moment comes. "He choked me, see there are still marks on my–" Molly tries to explain, but is cut off by her mother.

Jen shoves Molly behind her back, shushing her.

"Sorry officer, she doesn't know what she is talking about. Oh look he just pulled up." Jen says, holding Molly behind her back.

The officer turns and sees a truck pull into the side parking lot. The parking lot with all of the storage garages.

Jen bends down to Molly's face, "Don't say a thing. I don't want you to get taken." she says pointing her finger.

Molly feels her face become red. *He's right there, if I could just tell him what really happened we would both be out of all of this.* Her mind fights the voicelessness.

"But–" Molly tries again.

"No," Jen says firmly.

Smiling at the officer, assuring him that everything is *ok*.

Officers to the side begin talking to Nocens. Oddly enough, a few laughs break loose. Within minutes the officers begin to leave.

"Alright, looks like everything is good here. Have a good day ladies." an officer says, getting into his car.

"No–" she whispers.

Jen shoves her back a little more.

*Why are you stopping me from talking to them? It would get us both out of here.* Molly thinks confusingly.

Molly looks up at her mother, Jen looks away, refusing to make eye contact.

He touched her. He touched Molly. What's to stop him from gripping more than just her kneck?

"Why didn't you let me speak to those officers?" Molly asks.

"Because you don't know what really happened, and I can't stand the thought of losing you," her mother responds.

"I know what happened. He grabbed onto my kneck, and I couldn't breathe." water fills her eyes.

"Oh stop being so dramatic, he didn't want you to fall out of the car."

Molly can't help but giggle. *Keeping me from falling out of the car? You were between myself and the open door, you are the one who opened it in the first place. And most of all, you don't hold on to someone by the kneck to stop them from falling out of a moving car. I. Could. Not. Breathe.* She argues in her head but doesn't say a thing.

Noc had choked her, and Jen was defending him.

No matter what, Molly is not heard. She has never been. But now it is more than that, she isn't seen. If she can be suffocated and have marks left upon her body and nobody says a thing except for "be quiet". Then what could possibly make her be seen? Nothing, absolutely nothing.

Adults say that nothing can happen unless physical harm is being done. Is that not physical harm?

After everything, her own mother silenced her. Molly feels so helpless and vulnerable, it hurts.

She wonders if her voice would be better heard from a suicide letter. She wonders if the marks along her skin would be more recognized if the life was taken from her body. . .

Her mind is going crazy. So many thoughts racing upon her harmed mind.

All of the thoughts roll aside as she remembers soccer. The way the field makes her feel. How she can truly escape the world while she is playing the game. It is her own little world, her own little reality, and she couldn't imagine anything better.

She hangs onto the hope. Pushing aside all of the negative and painful emotions. None of it matters because she has hope. A positive belief that there will be more happiness, and she wants nothing more than to experience it. The thought of

*~ Passion From Within ~*

soccer, the thought of her own future family, all of it gives her hope and belief that there are better things in the world. More than what she is living. And that, that is what pulls her through late-night trembles, early morning fears, and all-day worries.

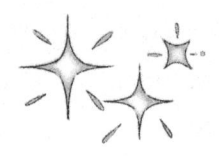

## Chapter 8

# What A Warrior Sees

Molly raises her hand, "Can I be the bubble gum guy?" she asks the teacher.

"Mm, no I have a better role for you." her teacher says, moving onto the next student.

*A better role? He is the main character, how could there be a better roll?* Molly wonders. Rubbing her fingers over the character sheet, over and over again until the wrinkles become soggy.

The room smells like crayons and crumbs leftover from the breakfast granola bars. Molly looks around, trying to avoid eye contact with her classmates. She has grown to be very shy. Instead, she looks at the harp sitting by the wall. Listening to the voices that surround her as the students pick the role they want in the upcoming Christmas play.

It has been 4 months since that day. The day she felt her body wither into thin air. The day she had been suffocated, by her mother's husband. They stayed in Metus until mid-August, then the three of them moved in with Molly's grandparents. Jen's parents. Nocens recently left, just last week. Picked up a job in a neighboring town, and is supposedly staying with a co-worker. Jen and Molly have been searching for places in their old town, Caput. There are nice places here and there, but it is taking a while to find the perfect one. Molly will be going back to her old elementary school for the other half of 3rd-grade. She is spending the first half at the elementary school near her grandparent's home.

After that day in Metus, things changed. Everyone was on edge and knew they had gone too far, though nobody said anything about it. Molly continued to question her mother for a while, but eventually stopped once she realized it was no use. Noc seemed fine when they first moved into her grandparent's home, but that soon came to an end. When both of her grandparents were gone, (which rarely happened) they would fight about anything and everything. It was like living with two siblings, except there was no adult supervision. Making Molly feel more grown than she was. She would be doing math homework, voices rose and objects fell. At one point, she called her grandparents and they came speeding back to the home. Relieving Molly, she would be at peace knowing that somebody else had seen what she was seeing. But that also was an overstatement, Noc and Jen were able to make everything look normal. Like usual.

~ *Riley Brett* ~

Molly has been enjoying her time away from Noc. Coming to her grandparent's home had made her nervous, because of Noc. She didn't want him to hurt either one of her grandparents. That would absolutely kill her, she would possibly attack him if he did so much as lay a hand on one of them.

When Noc and Jen moved in, Molly felt herself reach a more defensive side of herself. This was the one place she could always call home, no matter what. But once Noc came, that all changed. She no longer felt safe. She no longer felt comforted. And most importantly, she was fearful of her grandparents being harmed.

Now that Noc is gone, a piece of that worry has left. But she continues to be on guard, he now lives closer to her home. He knows exactly where she is, and that frightens her beyond words. And of course, she hasn't told anyone that she feels that way. Why would she? What could they possibly do? Call the police? Molly has already tried that, multiple times. It's no use. Even if there was something they could do, she wouldn't know what to say; "Hey I fear for our lives because Nocens lives near us.", yeah that would do a whole lot. They don't even know about the things that have happened in Metus. Why would anyone believe an eight-year-old who hasn't spoken about any of this before?

*Little does Molly know, warriors, vary between all ages, all races, and all kinds of opinions, everyone's voice, and story matters.*

"Molly. Did you hear me?" her teacher speaks up.

"Oh, um. No sorry," she says, trying to focus on the present.

"You will be Bellator. The warrior and savior of the town, basically you will be the hero. How does that sound?" the teacher gets closer to Molly, smiling convincingly.

"What? The savior? I am no savior, why would you have me as the savior?"

"Because I think you would suit the role well." she smiles even wider.

Molly tilts her head in confusion. *The savior. What does warrior even mean?* She tries to comprehend what her teacher had said.

"Ok. Thank you."

"Of course, now you will need to wear a very special outfit. We will talk more about it later." the teacher says, going on to talk to the rest of the class.

Molly smiles through the rest of the school day, antsy to get home and tell her grandparents the good news.

The day goes by extra slow.

"Papa!" Molly yells, running into her grandfather's arms.

His car is parked in front of the small elementary building.

"Hey, Molly! How was your day?" her Papa replies.

"It was great, I got one of the lead roles in the Christmas play!"

"Really? That's great. I can't wait to watch it."

She smiles back into his green eyes, seeing her reflection move in his eyes.

"Are you ready to go?"

"Yep." she hops into the car.

Tonight Molly goes to bed early, she is excited to start rehearsing for the play.

*The savior. A warrior.* The words travel through her head like a song on constant replay.

The question sits in her head all morning. Itching her mind, demanding to be answered.

"Hey Nana, I have a question," she says, painfully stuffing hot oatmeal into her mouth.

"Go ahead sweetie." her Nana replies.

"What does warrior mean?" she tilts her head, trying not to taste the plain oatmeal.

"Oh, that's a big word. Where did you hear that?" her Nana sets the morning paper down.

"At school. The teacher used it when she was talking about the role I will be in the school play."

"That sounds fun. It means a brave and experienced fighter or soldier."

"Oh." she stuffs more oatmeal into her mouth. Thinking deeply upon the definition, trying to understand.

Molly finishes her oatmeal and hurries through the house to get ready for school. Earlier and quicker than normal.

"What are you in a hurry for?" her Papa asks, walking around the corner of the bathroom entrance.

"I want to get to school and start rehearsals for the play." she brushes her teeth quickly, splashing toothpaste across the mirror and in the sink.

"Oh, I see. I will leave you to it. We leave in 5."

"O-k." she spits out the foaming paste. *Gross.*

Rushing through the morning she gets to school and sits in the morning room. She is the first one there. Waiting for everyone else to file in, eager to start play rehearsals.

She is happy to know what it means to be a warrior, though she doesn't fully understand it. The meaning itself is head tilting. Not because she doesn't get the meaning, but because she doesn't understand how it correlates with her. And why the teacher thinks it does.

Hours pass by until it is time to start rehearsals.

"Alright, class. Today we start going over our scripts. Now I ask that you practice your lines with a parent or sibling at home, at least 30 minutes a night. We will be practicing every day in school until the day comes, exactly two weeks from today. There will be two shows, one at lunch and one later at night." the teacher explains.

A day before Christmas break.

*Every night, for two weeks?* Molly's mind flusters. *Oh boy.*

"Let's begin. Open your packets up to page one, I would like for you to highlight your lines. They say who says what to the left of the lines. Highlighters are on the table in the front of the room." her teacher continues.

Molly studies her lines.

"Bellator."

As she drags the highlighter across her assigned lines she realizes how truly courageous and kind her character is. She questions why she was assigned this amazing roll.

"When you are all finished, we will start reading lines." her teacher says, interrupting Molly's thoughts.

Reading along the lines she experiences the character's deep thoughts also; worries, love, care, happiness, and so much more. Jumping between lines, she also realizes the conflict, who she will have to work against. Most of all, why she is fighting.

All of the character's emotions surface their lines. Telling who they are, not just as fictional characters but how it relates to reality.

Molly's face lights with the joy of the imminent events to take place.

Rehearsal continues on with line readings, talking out to the whole class, and role-playing.

. . .

The next few weeks consist much of the same. Along with very late nights, going over lines with her grandfather. He would read the other character's lines while Molly reads her own, acting and getting dramatic. Probably more than she needs to, but who's to tell an 8-year-old to not be so dramatic, *in a play*.

Early dreadful mornings go by slower than she could have expected. The weekend goes by even slower.

Molly, Jen, and her grandmother go shopping for her outfit. A beautiful outfit, for the perfect roll.

Jen calls all of Molly's relatives to let them know about the play; Sam, Albeny, and Horoma(her step-grandfather), and Dollan. Everyone has said they will make it to the night show.

. . .

~ *Passion From Within* ~

She has never experienced stage fright before. The closest thing to it would be the butterflies she gets before every soccer game, but that is much different. Soccer is familiar to her, she knows what to expect. As for a play, the only play she has been in was in kindergarten; 4 years ago. She doesn't remember much, other than the older kids dancing around in funny costumes and her teacher slapping a classmate. So far she isn't thrilled to take a second go at it.

Pacing back and forth behind the stage, her nerves go crazy. Her stomach has more than just butterflies, and her face is beyond red, it amounts to a ripe tomato.

She walks to the side of the stage, looking over the audience. There are many empty seats, yet she feels even more nervous.

"It's alright, you've got this." she whispers to herself. "Breathe. . . just breathe."

Her chest puffs with two big breaths of air.

Bellator characterizes Molly's body for the day. Her own personality is forgotten, just for the day, she acts as someone else; Bellator. In a white long sleeve shirt, a green t-shirt lays loosely over it. A green sparkly skirt puffs aside from her hips, shimmering in the light, making her ever so noticeable. Red and white striped tights fit snug around her small legs, leading down to her pointed green shoes. Completing the look will depend on how well she can play the role of *Bellator*. Kind, strong, ambitious, and joyful, but most of all a hero to his town's people.

"T-minus 5 minutes everyone." her teacher walks behind the stage.

Molly takes her last few looks over her script. Studying her lines, down to the last punctuation.

She hides her hands inside her long sleeves. Gripping onto the perfectly white long sleeves with her sweaty hands.

Her tongue shifts between her teeth, anxiously.

*Why does time have to move so slow?* She thinks, pacing behind the stage.

"Alright everyone, are you ready?" the teacher comes back.

Molly looks up, nervously. Her face sweating little beads along with the red pigment.

"Molly don't worry, you will do fine." her teacher puts her hand on Molly's shoulder and smiles into her red face.

Molly breathes deeply. Her face flushes slightly, her nerves settle. She is ready for the show.

"I am ready," she says, looking straight ahead, ready for the awaiting stage.

"Break a leg." the teacher releases Molly towards the stage.

Molly smiles at the comment. *I sure hope I don't.*

It's showtime.

The audience is dead silent as she walks along the steady stage, looking at all of the people in their positions. Ready for there *savior* to rescue them.

"Stop right there bubble gum Andy." Bellator enters the scene, prepared to save the innocent citizens of Gatum town from the villain. "You can not be mean to people. I will not let you."

"Oh really?" Bubble gum Andy responds, tough and angry.

"Yes," Bellator says firmly, yet kind.

"But they took my gum. They deserve what is coming to them." Bubble gum Andy pops his bubble gum.

"That is no reason to treat people poorly."

"Why should I listen to you? You are just some silly kid in a costume." the villain snarls.

"People are more than their appearances. I am more than my appearance." Bellator walks closer to Andy.

"Then how come you were so quick to call me the bad guy?" Andy shifts his head.

"Because of your actions. Your actions say more than words and appearances could ever say." Bellator says kindly.

"Ok, then what makes you so special?" Andy asks, circling Bellator.

"Nothing, I am just an ordinary kid trying to keep the town safe," Bellator states confidently.

"How can I be kind to people who have been mean to me?"

"You don't need to respond the way that they approached you. Stay true to yourself, and by doing that, you can be the best you. The kind you." Bellator gestures to Andy's heart

"Well, what if I don't want to?"

"Then that is up to you, but that is why we are talking and standing here. It isn't easy, I have gotten here by going through many trials. But in the end, I came out as a survivor and a warrior."

*Warrior.* It isn't someone who has necessarily been through a physical war. It is someone who has been through any war;

mental or physical. A warrior is someone who sees things through experience, reflects, and acts accordingly. Choosing to come out on the other side, getting through the battle, and not only surviving but thriving.

*It is what you do with the battle scars that matters most.* Molly feels the definition sink in, realizing its true meaning. Its true importance.

Bellator smiles at Bubble gum Andy, "Choose what side *you* want to come out on. It is up to you."

Bubble gum Andy shifts his feet, debating between his options." I don't want to be a villain, I was hurt. They hurt me, I wanted to get back at them, and I guess that wasn't the right way of doing things." he rubs his arms behind his back. "I choose to be the best that I can be, whatever that may be."

"We will be here to help you through it. All of us." Bellator smiles again, gesturing to the people all around him.

Bellator looks back at the citizens and feels relief, knowing he did the *best* that *he* could.

A reindeer walks up from behind Bellator and stands by his side for the closure of the play.

"Always be kind, no matter how rude others can be. Kindness doesn't hurt anyone, but being mean does. Choose your best self, choose your inner warrior." Bellator speaks out to everyone, taking the advice himself.

The play ends with Bellator's final words.

The crowd claps and cheers, echoing throughout the cafeteria walls.

~ *Passion From Within* ~

All of the kids' bow, then walk behind the stage.

*It is so much more than just a play.* Molly realizes. *I hope to be as brave as Bellator someday.* She thinks, walking to her assigned spot backstage. Throughout everything she has been through, she is the person in her own way. The one who stops herself from telling anyone about what truly goes on when she is alone with her *guardians*.

She mutes herself. And she doesn't even know it.

A bigger question is, why? Why does she mute herself?

She doesn't like feeling or being voiceless. So why would she do it to herself?

All warriors have flaws, even fears, and worries. The only difference between a warrior and someone rather different is the resilience they obtain. How they can persevere through a crying battle, and come out the other side stronger. The simplest key to finding that light, that resilience, is understanding that you will be at your absolute weakest in the battle, only knowing you will come out stronger. Denying the possibility of growing weaker. Resilience feeds off of battle, and the scars that live within those battles. The soldier gets to choose whether or not to mend the scars and tell the gory stories, or to leave it, and try to forget it had ever happened. Though the scar will insist to be remembered if left open, it will ache and throb, screaming to be helped. It is up to the soldier, the fighter, to give the scar the tools it needs to heal and recover stronger than it would have been without the sharp gash.

...

At the night show, there is a much bigger crowd. The entire cafeteria is packed, people are spilling into the hall.

Molly peaks her head around the wall trying to find her family. She makes eye contact with her Papa and smiles. Continuing to scan the room she sees Albeny, Horoma, her father(Sam), her Nana, and her mother. Everyone, but Dollan.

Her nerves leap again. This time out of anger and sadness, not stage-fright.

She digs her fingernails into her palms, trying to alleviate the frustration.

"T-minus 5 minutes." the teacher says, walking behind the stage.

Molly takes a deep breath and continues through the final show. Watching her family almost the entire time, finding comfort within their eyes.

After the show, she runs up to her father(Sam) and hugs him tightly. Getting glitter all over him.

"Hey, sweety!" her father squeezes her tightly. He gives the absolute best hugs.

"Hey dad!" she replies, "You came," she says softly, gripping tighter.

"Of course I did. I couldn't miss your big show." Sam says, continuing to hug her tightly. "I am so proud of you." he says more softly.

Molly feels a smile pick up her cheeks. "Thank you." her heart leaps with warmth.

Sam loosens his grip, "How have you been?"

A recent memory flashes through her mind. . .

*Molly and her mother lay on the couches in the basement of her grandparent's house, watching their favorite TV series. It is only Molly and her mom, her grandparents are in town getting groceries.*

*A loud noise comes from outside.*

*"What was that?" Molly asks her mom.*

*"I'm sure it was nothing. It's fine." Jen replies, continuing to focus on the TV screen.*

*Molly looks over towards the staircase, feeling her gut-wrench.*

*She ignores the sound and focuses on the TV.*

*"Jen." a deep voice says from the top of the stairs.*

*Jen gets off of the couch cautiously. "Hello?" she says, walking over to the bottom of the stairs.*

*"Mom, be careful," Molly says, getting off the couch and following her.*

*"Molly, stay back." Jen says quietly. "Who is it?"*

*Jen turns her head up the stairs. "Jeez, why didn't you call?"*

*"I need to speak with you." the voice says firmly.*

*Molly disobeys her mother and runs to her side. She gasps at the figure standing in the doorway.*

*"Hey, Moll." Nocens says. "Listen to your mother, go sit down."*

*"Stay here Molly, I'll be back," Jen says, walking towards the stairs.*

*"Mom, no." Molly pleads.*

*"It will be fine." Jen walks up the stairs.*

*Molly feels her heart sink. Fear fills her aching stomach.*

*Voices rise from upstairs and the door slams. . .*

The memory fades, "Good, I missed you." Molly says, not speaking up for herself, *once again.*

"Good, I have missed you too." Sam replies, handing her flowers. "For you."

She grabs the beautiful, and sweet-smelling flowers. "Thank you, Dad."

"Of course. That was a great performance."

She smiles, comforted by him being here.

"Molly! That was a great performance." more relatives come walking over to congratulate her.

The night passes by quickly, too quickly. Before she knows it she is saying goodbye to her father and the rest of her relatives.

"Bye sweety, it was great seeing you. I love you." Sam says, getting into his car to head back home.

"Bye Dad, I love you too," Molly replies, in the cold winter air. Feeling her breath fog in front of her eyes. Her voice stays captive inside of her throbbing gut, wishing to be heard. More importantly, wishing she had the bravery to voice her feelings and what has truly happened.

She gets into their car and warms her cold hands. The memory finds its way back. . .

*Molly runs up the basement stairs and to the front door.*

*Voices rise from outside. She watches out the glass door, as Nocens presses up against Jen who is sitting in her driver's seat with the door open.*

"Get away Nocens. Leave me alone!" Jen sobs, pulling her arms around herself trying to protect herself from the impact of his dangerous hands.

Molly watches with needles in her eyes. Poking until tears pour from her throbbing tear glands. "I have to call somebody, he's going to hurt her," she says to herself.

She runs to the living room and gets the house phone, she dials her Papa's number. Praying that he will pick up.

"Grandpa! Can you. . . can you come home? Nocens is here and I think he is hurting mom." Molly tries her very best to hold back the tears.

Her Papa doesn't hesitate for a second, "We will be right there, stay up in our room, ok?" he says.

"Ok." she stutters, hearing the phone beep to an end." Please hurry. . ." she whispers into the silent phone.

Every part of her body collapses, starting at the knees. Folding onto the floor, water spilling into a puddle within the carpet. Her hands shake aggressively, in sadness more than anything. She tries to breathe through her stuffed nose, but it only makes her shed more tears.

Worries cloud her thoughts, and she stands to the window. Trying to see what is going on. The roof over the front entrance blocks her view of the truck, where Jen had been sitting. No matter what angle she tries to look from, she can't see her mother.

Molly is clueless, all she can do is sit and wait for her grandparents. The suspense makes time pass torturously, seconds ticking by as if they were minutes, and minutes like hours.

*Until finally, after what seems like hours, a car pulls up the driveway and two people get out. It's her grandparents. Relief settles her shaky hands.*

*She yells out of their bedroom window, "You've been caught Nocens."*

*Finally, someone saw what he had done for so long. She runs down the stairs and stands at the front door, hesitating. Her saviors are here, yet she feels oddly unsafe and scared.*

*The sound of a motorcycle starts up and speeds off. He's gone.*

*She runs outside to confront everyone and see what they did about it. "Hey, is he going to jail? Are they going to catch him?"*

*"No Molly. Nothing actually happened." her mother says, her eyes dry as if she hadn't been crying.*

*"What? But I saw him, he was—"*

*"-Nothing happened, he just needed to talk and it actually went well."*

*"But—"*

*"Molly. I am sorry that it scared you, though nothing happened." Jen says sternly.*

*Her jaw drops, but her lips stay closed. He was all over her, and she was yelling for him to stop. Molly knows what she saw, and it was frightening to her young mind. Nobody can take that feeling from her, it will stay there for years to come.*

The memory ends, as they pull up their dark driveway.

. . .

She spends multiple days struggling to figure out who she is or who she wants to be. A thought that will not leave her mind is how the meaning of a warrior could correlate with her. How could she possibly be a warrior? What battle has she fought, and has she won or lost?

Those questions repeat themselves over and over in her mind, day by day. Thankfully it is Christmas Day tomorrow, which is her favorite holiday. Only because she gets to use it as a reason to hang out with *all* of her family members, at once. She can forget about everything, just for two days.

The Christmas tree looks beautiful this year. It is full of shimmering ornaments and colorful lights. The tree sits directly to the right of the fireplace, where 6 vibrant stockings hang. Sitting along the shelf above the fireplace, there are glass decorations; reindeer, snowmen, and a Santa Claus. On the Tv stand to the left of the fireplace, shimmering red decor hangs along its edges. Cinnamon fills the air, and hot chocolate layers their mouths.

Wonderous curiosity sits upon her mind, questioning what is in the wrapped boxes under the tree. Most of all, hoping her family will like the presents that she made for each of them. A variety of colors lay beneath the tree, waiting to be taken off of its tagged gift.

Christmas Eve is full of delicious food and endless laughs.

"Molly open that big one right there." her papa says, pointing to a large gift sitting by the fireplace. "It's from uncle Virtus."

~ *Riley Brett* ~

It is a big present in the shape of a right triangle. What could it possibly be?

She rips it open and her jaw drops in awe. Picking it up out of the box, she rubs her fingers along its smooth surface. Admiring its creative potential.

It's a guitar.

Pink and ever so shiny.

"Wow." her jaw still dropped." It's. . . it's amazing," she says, turning it over and examining its perfectly polished edges.

Uncle Virtus is Jen's younger brother, by two years. Molly is close to him but they never seem to live close to one another. He takes her on crazy adventures whenever they get the chance, he is her wild side. She couldn't be more thankful to have an uncle like him.

. . .

The rest of the evening continues with present opening and munching on leftovers from dinner. It is a wonderful night, full of family bonding and endless joy. Having all of her family together makes everything feel more than just bearable, enjoyable.

Darkness settles into the sky, making the shimmering lights give off even more vibrant light. That being said, Christmas Eve soon comes to an end, now awaiting Christmas day and the adventures set for the pleasant holiday.

. . .

Morning comes with comfort and long-lasting yawns. It is the one day when everyone stays in their PJ's for an extra hour.

*~ Passion From Within ~*

The one day when Molly can run around the house with her fluffy blanket wrapped around her neck like a cape, pretending she is a super-hero and she can take on the world. Sparking a flare of the inner warrior, warming her veins of excitement. The joy of overcoming battles, and entering the other side stronger than any villain could ever dream to be.

She continues to run around the morning, flying with her cape into the next few moments in time. . .

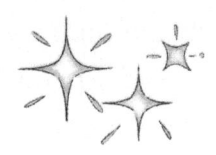

## Chapter 9
# Safe Haven

After Christmas, things went by quickly. Jen found a place for them to rent back in Caput. A very nice house, a few blocks from Molly's elementary school she will be attending for the second half of 3rd grade, and a few blocks further from T.

Snow still coats the ground, far up north all the way down south. Leftover Christmas lights brighten the streets during the night. Falling snowflakes shimmer underneath the street lights, colliding one after another.

Goodbyes are always so difficult. Though it isn't truly "a final goodbye", she will see them again, at least she hopes to. The thought crosses her mind every time she has to leave them. . .

"Bye Molly, I love you so so much. Call us when you get there, alright?" her nana says, hugging Molly tightly.

"Ok Nana, I will." Molly grips onto her grandmother." I love you too." she whispers, hugging her grandmother even tighter.

A kiss lays atop of Molly's forehead, her Nana releases her from the tight hug, and smiles.

"Papa. . ." Molly says quietly, her heart drops, butterflies fly chaotically around her stomach.

She runs into his arms, not squeezing tightly. Instead, she just feels his safeguarding body hug her protectively. Her hands intertwine with each other behind his back, hoping this moment will last forever. Hoping that if she holds on tight enough, she could slow time down, and never have to say bye. If only the hug could create its own infinity, and be everlasting. Only if his hug could truly protect her from the entire world, his hug could shield her from a fire breathing dragon, his hug could make absolutely anything possible. If only. . .

"I love you, sweetie. You are going to do great, and we will come to visit, I promise." he grips onto her, alleviating her of the pain as if he physically took the pain and put it on himself. Taking the pain away that he isn't even aware of.

"Do you pinky promise?" she asks, holding back the tears that rip down her throat.

He sticks out his pinky, and hooks it into hers, "I pinky promise."

She quickly releases his pinky, and hugs him one last time. "You are the best grandpa in the whole wide world, and I love you." her throat throbs and aches.

Little sniffles come from her stuffed button nose.

"I love you so much Molly." he squeezes onto her, one last time.

*I can't even put into words how much I love you. How leaving you makes my heartache. How leaving you makes my gut hurt. How leaving you makes me feel like. . .feel like I am losing my strength to persevere.* She thinks about her grandfather. Understanding that he has been more of a father to her than a grandpa. Understanding that leaving him causes her an amount of pain that she will never be able to put into words. Understanding that he doesn't know. . . he doesn't know all that has happened, and why that makes him her *safe haven*.

"Ready Molly?" Jen asks from in the car.

Molly loosens her grip, feeling her fingers slide away from each other, "Yeah." she says softly.

"We will see you guys soon." her Papa says as she gets into the car.

"I love you both! Good luck." her Nana adds, smiling and waving as their car rolls down the gravel driveway.

"Goodbye. . ." she whispers, putting her hand against the cold window. "see you soon." her words cause the cold window to fog before her eyes.

The site of her grandparents slowly fades as they turn the corner. Molly feels a sadness sweep over her, making her body ache. Tears proceed to threaten her eyes, but she doesn't give in, she holds them back. Feeling her throat close tightly from the pressure of the tears.

*It's fine, everything will be ok.* Molly tries to convince herself. *At least we will be living far from Nocens. But what if Nocens decides to do something to them? What if he hurts them?* Worries continue to flood her mind, for what seems like weeks to come.

. . .

Her worries settle as time goes on. Happiness makes its way back into their lives, slowly.

The house they are renting has more room than she expected. Time goes on, a lot of it being with T. Molly and T spend so much time together they basically live with one another. It comforts her to know that she has somebody by her side, no matter what. She can't say the same about her school life. Things have changed so drastically, bullies have gotten far worse. Telling her to "go kill yourself", or "nobody likes you, why are you even here?", and so much more. Molly finds a side of herself that she never wants to see again, a side where she fights back. Not in a good way, the anger fills her fists and makes her feel out of control. She has already gotten in 2 other fights throughout elementary school, fistfights to be specific. This one was her third, with someone who she had no intention of hurting, but the pain that she was feeling demanded to be felt and she wasn't able to control herself. She swung her fist angrily and instantly felt regret, as she looked into the other person's eyes, seeing the pain that she had just caused them. Realizing that the answer to her own pain isn't causing somebody else pain. Empathy made her feel even worse than she did before she threw the hit, after that she promised herself she would never hurt somebody like that ever again. Promising herself that she would try to understand the other person rather than fight them over a disagreement.

After that fight, Molly didn't get bullied again, even if she did it was nowhere as bad as it was before. Because of that, she was able to finish elementary school happily. Everything was close to perfect, Molly hasn't felt that in so long. Summer began with sleepovers with T, movie nights with her mom, beaches, and so much more. But most of all, she had fun, the summer was starting out wonderfully. She even won 3rd place in playoffs, on a u12 team, which was huge for her because she just turned 9. Everything made her so unbelievably happy, it almost seemed unreal. Until today...

. . .

"So, I thought that I would let you know that Noc will be at the 4th of July party," her mother says cautiously.

Molly looks away from the window, "What?" she asks, hoping she misheard her mother.

"Yeah, it's his parent's party and they invited him. You don't have to go, but you already told Annie that you would be there."

"I, um. We are already on our way, so I don't exactly have a choice." her mind is in shock.

*I thought I would never have to see him again. I don't know if I can face him, not after everything that has happened.* Molly thinks fearfully.

"Yeah. It will be alright, just please be good, we are guests."

*Are you serious?* She thinks angrily. "Sure."

She can't tell who she is angrier with, her mom or Nocens.

. . .

Let's just say it went exactly how you thought it would. Noc started coming over as Jen's "friend". But of course it never just stays at that...

Molly lays in their guest bedroom reading out of her book, preparing for this coming school year which begins in a week. The door is cracked, with enough visibility of the hallway.

Voices raise in her mother's room right across the hall, more intense than she is used to.

Her head tilts in confusion. She walks to her door to see what is going on. Jen and Nocens are sitting on her mother's bed. Everything is fine, just a disagreement. Molly lays back down and closes her eyes.

Following a few minutes later, the stairs begin to creek. Molly's heart beats faster, in the fear of familiarity. Her gut knows what will happen before they do.

She walks to the door slowly, peeking her head between the small crack.

Jen is backing up down the stairs, slowly and cautiously. Watching every move Noc makes. Cries release from her mother's body, "I thought we weren't going to do this again... you promised me that things would be different and that we would just be friends." Jen's voice shakes in a plead.

"Well, I changed my mind. We can never be just friends." Noc says firmly, with an evil leer.

Everything happens so fast... he leaps for her vulnerable body and slams it against the wall.

Molly's skin trembles. She quietly shuts her bedroom door and locks the deadbolt. *No, please not again.* She thinks, fearing what almost seems inevitable.

More clashes come from down the hall, her mother's body lets out more cries and weeps.

Molly steps back from the door, in complete shock. Things have not changed, and they never will. Her body rides with fear, stabbing into her scared gut. So much fear lives within her heart, her blood, her skin, her everything.

As more clashes come from downstairs, Molly's body becomes weak and she collapses to the floor, feeling the tears splash upon the hardwood floor. Emptiness fills her stomach, realizing there is nothing she can do. If she called anyone Nocens would make up an excuse for what he is doing to her mother's body. Nobody would listen to the frightened 9-year-old sitting in her dark bedroom soaked in tears. Nobody would care what the scared little girl has to say, because she isn't an adult and "*doesn't understand half of it.*"

Cries echo throughout the walls, beating down any chance to make happy memories. Taking away all hope to have a better life. Making it impossible to forget about the chills she feels sitting in this room tonight.

Her weak vulnerable body sits along the wet hardwood floor, hoping her mother isn't in pain, wishing she could help her. Wishing she could do anything but sit here and be completely helpless.

As the night goes on, the cries grow weaker. . . until finally, they stop. Molly prays to god that her mother is ok, more specifically that she is alive.

Horrific fear still rides along Molly's skin, making it impossible to do anything. She is so frightened that when she realizes she has to go pee, she uses the garbage can. Gross, but safer than going out there.

Her body continues to tremble throughout the night. Shaking aggressively with sadness, and fear of what he could have done to Jen.

The look in her mother's eyes. It completely broke Molly to see her mother like that. Looking deep into her frightened body, she looked as if she knew what was going to happen and that there was nothing she could have done about it. The only other person in the house is Molly, and when she calls the police nothing happens.

Molly lays awake for what seems like hours, unable to calm the chill that lays intensely along her skin. Shaking and trembling, in complete shock. Hoping that the lock on the door could hold if he were to try and break-in. She lays there wondering if he will try to knock the door down, she wonders so deeply about it that it feels like it is actually happening. Her body curls into a ball, rocking itself to comfort. If only she could still be in her grandfather's arms, in the arms of her *safe haven.*

. . .

~ Riley Brett ~

Sunlight spreads across her face, making her eyes ache. Her eyes are red and watery, her nose is still stuffed and hard to breathe through.

*Mom.* The first thought of the morning pops into her mind.

She slowly gets out of bed, feeling her body throb as she stands to her feet. Wobbling back and forth, she is able to eventually steady herself.

Walking to the door, her shaking hand reaches the cool metal lock, and twists. The door opens and lets in darkness from the horrifying hallway.

A deep breath fills her body and settles her chills. *It will be ok, you've got this. Don't worry, it will be fine. Just breathe, mom needs you.* Her thoughts travel along her struggling mind. She walks down the hall, cautiously and steadily, trying not to make a sound.

Little creeks come from the floorboards beneath her feet, she flinches at the thought of him being downstairs. She proceeds despite the fear, reaching the spot where her mother had been just last night while backing down the stairs. Her heart drops, sadness splashes through her eyes. *It's fine, she is fine.* She takes a deep breath, trying to convince herself that everything will be alright.

She steps slowly down each stair, only a few creeks after each step. Her head peeks around the corner, feeling the fear of who could be there. But it is only her mother, she is laying on the couch, alone.

She now runs down the stairs, lightly on her feet. Standing in front of her mother, she sees her nude body lying beneath a small blanket. Bruises placed along her fair skin.

Molly covers her mouth in horror. Jen's body is weak and vulnerable, reminding Molly of the days at their old place when she was 4.

*He... did he? Did he rape her?* Her thoughts tear at her eyes and skin, making her feel unsafe and scared.

"Mom..." she says softly, "mom, mom wake up."

No response.

Molly moves closer to her mother's body and nudges her arm, "Mom, please wake up..."

Jen rolls her body over, opening her eyes and quickly covering her body. She sits up quickly, not saying a thing.

"Are you alright?" Molly asks.

"Yeah... yeah, I'm fine." Jen replies softly. "Why wouldn't I be?" she looks up at Molly as if nothing happened.

Molly feels the pain sink deeper, it hurts more since her mother won't talk about it like it happened. She knows it happened, lying about it makes it far worse.

She shakes her head, she leaves her mother and checks out the rest of the house. Making sure that he is really gone.

When she checks upstairs she finds a letter in her mother's room, it's from him. A notebook paper, shaggy, and full of threats. Reading along the lines, she is frightened in every way possible. *When will it end, it has to end.* The last bit of hope leaves.

"What is that?" Jen asks walking into the room with a blanket wrapped around her.

"It's a letter from Nocens." Molly looks into her mother's eyes, frightened and concerned.

"Let me see."

Molly hands Jen the letter and watches her facial expression change as she lips the words.

When she finishes, her eyes are slightly watered but she would never let Molly see her cry if she had control of it. "Don't worry, I am going to be getting a restraining order and a divorce." she says saddened, yet firmly. "I'm going to call a friend to come to stay with you while I go to the courthouse to take care of this."

"What no. Please don't leave, what if he comes back?" her eyes begin to water again.

"You'll be fine, he wouldn't hurt you even if he did come back."

*I still have the feeling of his arm around my kneck, keeping me from breathing. Yeah. . . you're right he won't hurt me.* She remembers the feeling she had in that truck, that hot and frightening truck. How his bicep flexed around her kneck, just enough to block oxygen.

. . .

The rest of the day blurs by, she is so on edge that she can't even sit down. Her body shakes continuously while her mother is gone and even when she gets back. Oddly enough the restraining order sheet was easy, but the divorce will take longer.

Crazy how they truly were *fabricated vows.*

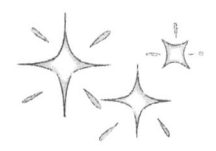

## Chapter 10

# What The Future May Hold

"Molly I want you to meet somebody, this is Loyd. He is a high school friend of mine." Jen says, standing in their kitchen next to a muscular man.

"Hello," Molly replies with a small smile.

"Hi, it's nice to meet you." Loyd greets her with a genuine smile.

*He is very muscular, he could definitely take on Nocens in a fight.* She thinks, sizing him up.

It has been not even a week since Jen got the restraining order on Nocens. Molly hasn't seen him since and prays not to.

"I heard you play soccer. Are you in a season right now?" Loyd continues.

~ *Riley Brett* ~

"Yeah, I am in my fall season. We have our playoffs games this weekend actually," she replies, happy that she can talk about something she loves.

"That's cool, I played sports as a kid, I know all about it. I didn't play soccer but I played football."

"That's cool. Please tell me you are a fan of the Orsus team."

"Of course I am! I could never be a Caput fan." Loyd chuckles.

Molly has been a football fan for as long as she can remember, starting with the influence of her grandfather. Yelling at the TV screen every football Sunday.

"Good." she joins him in laughter. "I am going to go play with T if that's ok mom?"

"Yeah, go ahead," Jen replies.

"Ok thanks, it was nice meeting you Loyd." She leaves the house with a kind smile on her face. Maybe there is hope after all, for her mother's happiness. For a man to make her happy, she just wishes it to be true.

. . .

The whistle blows and the ball rolls to Molly. "Push up," Molly yells to her team.

Feeling the ball tap at her feet gives her happiness that settles into her veins. Thriving and embracing through everything that causes her pain.

She passes up the field and runs into open space, creating options towards the net.

Grass flies in the air.

## ~ Passion From Within ~

Sweat drips from her tired body.
BO fills her nose.
Bruises form along her throbbing skin.
Thick saliva layers her mouth.

Her aching legs rip and sprint down the field, gripping onto the grass. Every part of her body begging for water amongst the hot and humid day. She pulls her jersey to her face and feels the breeze brush along her sweaty stomach, her lungs breathe in the sweet warm air. Every single moment of the game brings her joy and purpose.

Sweat drips into her eyes as she looks up the field, shaking her head as it flies off her face. She does tiny jumps on her toes, gaining energy throughout her body. Warming up her inner beast, her inner warrior. Preparing herself for the game she loves so dearly, the game she is so severely passionate about, the game that shows her who she truly is and who she could be. Creating a thriving *passion from within*.

"Here," she points in front of her right foot, "I'm open!" her sore legs sprint into space.

Receiving the ball at her blistering feet, she looks up and scans her options. Space opens between the two defenders in front of her, she runs forward tapping the ball at her feet creating the ever so amazing music to her ears. A quick fake one way and a body check another way. She weaves through the last players and shoots, swishing the ball into the back of the net.

Jumping up, she cheers for her heart-filled goal. Her team runs to her and taps her on the back or gives a high-five.

## ~ Riley Brett ~

Looking over to the parents she tries to find her mom, scanning, and scanning until she sees a woman sitting on a blanket next to a man. It's her, with Loyd.

Instead of being mad, she gets even happier. Not many people have cared enough to come to her games, especially not important games. A smile spreads between her hot sweaty cheeks.

Along the side-line, before she looks away she watches her mother and Loyd clap in celebration of her goal. She has fans. People who care to watch her do what she is best at, soccer.

. . .

Weeks go by, full of fun times and many sleepovers. Things have been going very well, yet she is full of worries and fear. Finding her voice continues to be hard, time after time she feels closer to finding it, but it never stays. The bravery always tends to fade. It is an everyday struggle that she continues to fight and push through, all she cares about for right now is the time being and how things are in the very moment. She has no idea what the future holds, and she never has. But now more than ever, she is fighting to keep the peace, comfort, safety, and happiness that is present now. Hoping every night that it could stay like this forever, not knowing how horrible things could possibly get, how drastically things could change because after all, she is nine years old and still has a lot to learn. Every day goes on being a mystery, but that isn't anything new. That is one thing life can always guarantee, you will never know what is to come next and in regards to that, the only thing that you can control is how you prepare yourself for an unpromising future.

~ *Passion From Within* ~

. . .

Molly coats her face with a cold light green face mask, T does the same. Both of them look like zombies; their eyes tired and droopy, their arms listless, and their face covered in green. A newly released movie plays on Molly's TV, they laugh and make jokes as the film goes on. Eating popcorn and throwing it at one another.

"We should watch another scary movie after this!" Molly says excitedly.

"No, I think we shouldn't." T laughs, she is not a huge fan of horror films.

"Why not, they are fun to watch together. Pleaseee?" she begs.

"No are you kidding, at night? You must be out of your mind." T giggles while taking her mask off.

"True, we can watch one tomorrow, when it is light outside."

"Ok, fine. And we can order Chinese food." T smiles.

"Great idea!"

Molly shoves more popcorn into her mouth, crunching on its buttery goodness. Then eats more sour candy, it is almost a tradition for Molly and T to have a movie night on Saturdays. Eating popcorn, doing masks, watching a new movie, and most of all the candy which is a secret they will never share.

They both fall asleep earlier than they plan for, the comfy blankets tend to get the best of them. Sleeping through the night they roll and shift over the popcorn lying on the bed sheets, crunching with every turn. . .

~ *Riley Brett* ~

*Darkness fills the whole house. Dim only in the corners with broken lamps.*

*The house is full of clear gross tarps, hanging down from the ceilings. Everything feels off, unsafe, and deadly. Chills ride along her skin, itching from within her bones. Someone shifts across the room, a shadow of fear. Molly creeps up the stairs, trying to find her mother.*

*"Mom? Mom are you here?" her voice echoes as if it will never stop. Ringing and ringing off the beaten walls.*

*She grabs onto her sides with both of her hands, wrapping herself into a hug, hoping to comfort her chills. Green goo leaks from the ceiling and down the walls.*

*"Where am I?" she whispers to herself.*

*A sound comes from in her mother's room, she walks cautiously down the dark and narrow hall. The sound becomes louder. As she reaches the room she peeks her head in, hoping to find her mother. All she finds is the TV grey and white, making a static noise.*

*"Weird," she says again.*

*Jen's sheets are wrinkled as if someone had been lying there. A dent sinking into the bed as if they had just left.*

*"Molly! Molly! Where are you?" Molly hears Jen's voice screaming down the hall.*

*"Mom! Mom?" she runs down the hall towards the noise, suddenly the hall shrinks and becomes even more narrow. She sprints, clashing along the walls and tripping over her own feet, yelling and screaming for her mother.*

*In the bathroom there is a steel sink, resting with rust along its edges. A clear curtain drapes over the deep tub, a body rests against* the curtain pushing along its clear surface. The room is too dark to tell who it is or what they are doing, all she can see is a figure, lying unlively.

"Mom?" she says softly, stepping closer.

Her heart tenses with the question that repeats in her mind.

The figure shifts, rocking. Then suddenly stops. Causing Molly to stop mid-step.

"Mom is that you?" she asks again, her voice shaking.

She pulls the curtain aside, and there lies Jen's body; grey and unlively. Her eyes staring up at the ceiling, still green but heartless. No warmth or comfort radiating off of her, no assurance that everything will be ok.

Molly leaps back, gasping for air. Every part of oxygen from her body leaves into the toxic room. Her body shaking and trembling over her mother's body, it is her but something is different. She can't tell what it is. Tears drip down her shaking cheeks.

"Mom. . . mom, please wake up, you're ok. . . you'll be ok." she collapses to the floor still shaking with disbelief.

Another object shifts through the halls. Making Molly's heart clench.

"He. . . hello?" she stutters.

It moves again. The hall is too dark, and it seems as if it is getting darker. . . moments go by as Molly steps closer to the entrance of the bathroom. Step after step, creek after creek.

A thud comes from within Jen's room. . . seconds go by like hours until it is almost completely dark. Molly scans her eyes along the ceiling and the walls, feeling another presence fill the house, a *breath, a heart beating, a person. She can sense the breath coming from its body.*

*Someone runs towards Molly, making everything go completely black. . .*

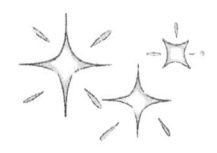

# Character Meanings

Important characters within the story have names unique to their best trait. Listed below are their name from in the story and the English definition of the Latin word the name comes from.

Main character—Molly—based on the Latin word Mollitiam, meaning resilient.

The cat—Salvus—based on the Latin word Salvus, meaning alive, safe, and sound.

The grandmother/mother's mom—Nana/Fidum—based on the Latin word Fidum, meaning dependable, loyal, faithful, and confident.

The grandfather/mother's father—Papa/Solat—based on the Latin word Solatium, meaning comfort, relief, soothing.

~ Riley Brett ~

The grandmother/bio father's mother—Albeny/grandma—based on the Latin word Bonum, meaning good and gift.

The grandfather/bio father's father—Horoma—based on the Latin word Horoma, meaning vision.

The mother—Mom/Jen—based on the Latin word Genus, meaning kind, and noble birth.

The dad—Dollan/bio-dad—based on the Latin word Dolor, meaning smart and heartache.

The *father*—Samuel/dad—based on the Latin word Sophus, meaning sage/Wiseman.

The uncle/mother's brother—Virtus/uncle v—based on the Latin word Virtus, meaning valor and good quality.

The aunt—Tia—based on the Latin word Intantia, meaning perseverance and vehemence.

The older brother—Samuel Jr/Little Sam—based on the Latin word Sophus, meaning sage/Wiseman.

The little sister—Cassity—based on the Latin word Castitas, meaning purity and innocence.

The step sister—Annie—based on the Latin word Animus, meaning heart, purpose, and bravery.

The cousins/bio father's nieces and nephews—Gloria—based on the Latin word Gloria, meaning honor and ambition.

Lae—based on the Latin word Laetita, meaning joy and delight.

Cora—based on the Latin word Cor, meaning heart.

The best friend—Tutela/T—based on the Latin word Tutela, meaning protection, care and safeguard.

The mother's boyfriend—Nocens/Noc—based on the Latin word Nocens, meaning hurtful and culpable.

Relations who will not be named—

Loyd—based on the English word Loyalty, meaning a feeling of support and allegiance.

**Geographic Names:**

Country—Votum—based on the Latin word Votum, meaning hope and aspiration.

Towns—Orsus—based on the Latin word Orsus, meaning beginning.

Solatium—based on the Latin word Solatium, meaning comfort.

Caput—based on the Latin word Caput, meaning civil existence and chapter.

Metus—based on the Latin word Metus, meaning fear and dread.

# About The Author

Riley Brett is the author of historical fiction, Passion From Within. She was 15 years old when it got published. So far some of her accomplishments include, playing high school soccer and participating in debate, all in her hometown, Duluth, MN. The book was written during a world-wide pandemic and a summer visit to Florida. The book was written in hopes that it will raise awareness to those who go unheard and unseen, the story isn't just for entertainment it is a resource for those who beg to have their voices heard.

Read more on her author website: Passionfromwithin.org

Made in the USA
Monee, IL
05 November 2020